$E_1$

*Epithalamium*

*Epithalamium*

*Are God and Nature then at strife,*
*That Nature lends such evil dreams?*
*So careful of the type she seems,*
*So careless of the single life;*

- 'In Memoriam A.H. H.', Lord Alfred Tennyson, 1849

*Epithalamium*

# 1

Julian can hear their cries as clearly now in his mind as when he first heard them. Shrill voices, fractured by the crushing weight of fear.
Terrified.
Begging.
He licks his dry lips, regrets it immediately. They sting. An icy gust blows at them, making them sing with pain. Instinctively he runs his tongue over them again, trying to protect them against the biting chill and only making it worse. Perpetuating his suffering.
'I said are you okay?'
The voice is harsh and annoyed. Each word was over-pronounced like the speaker is talking to an idiot.
Julian's eyes refocus. The cries in his mind retreat to the back of it, albeit only for a small time he knows. Through the drifting flakes an obnoxious white glare of LED headlights set at too high an angle. Another gust sent the flakes into a swirling dance. Movement beyond them, a sigh.
A face is staring at him, skin cracked with age with eyes narrowed, a tall, liver-spotted brow furrowed in irritation. A pair of hand jerked, palms open, inviting a response.
'David, get back in the car'. Another voice. This one from inside the car, female and Julian eyes snap to her, 'He's clearly not with it. Leave him and let's get home before the roads seize up'
David doesn't move, his gaze locked on Julian. He speaks again, louder, but this time with genuine concern, 'Do you need help?'

## *Epithalamium*

Julian's heart begins to pound and he squints through the fluttering white particles and the misty glare of the headlamps. A woman sits in the passengers' seat, her own gaze shifting from Julian to David and back again. Light hair and blue eyes, this much only he could discern in the gloom. Julian cranes his neck and raises his hand to block out the dazzling white.

'What are you looking at?' David's tone has now lost its empathy, replaced with a territorial terseness. Julian knows it well. He'd used it many times. Right now, however, all his attention was focused on the woman in the car staring back at him.

Julian steps forward, trying to find a position where the painful light projected at him was diminished. Orange light pulses at the side of his face, from the corners of his own car beside him.

*Blue eyes. Light hair. Good.*

Excitement and fear collide in the pit of his stomach.

The weight in the back of his waistband increases tenfold and his legs feel suddenly weaker.

With his left hand, he manages to block some more light.

*A narrow chin. High cheekbones. Promising.*

Julian's right-hand moves around his back to his sagging leather belt and his fingers wrap around the pistol's grip, pulling slightly, easing the burden.

David watches him and Julian can somehow feel the tension rise, even across the several yards that separate them on the quiet road.

The isolation of that stretch of broken tarmac has suddenly become all too apparent. A half mile from junction to junction, one ahead and one behind. Parallel to them was a dual carriageway, the hissing of the passing heavy traffic squeezing

*Epithalamium*

between the dark factories and warehouses between it and them.

Davids hand on the top of the door moves. Clearly, in his late 70's, it was obvious that he wasn't a man who was easily scared but had endured into his golden years by having a keen instinct for danger, and a blend of intuition and experience hard won by those gathering winters. He was about to make a primal decision.

Fight or flight.

In her seat, the woman leans forward a little. The mist of oppressive light clears a little and Julian can finally make out her face.

*Lines.*

Dried up rivers and tributaries cut across an undulating expanse of time-weathered skin. Her papery complexion a shadow of former beauty lost to all but those who knew her in her glorious youth.

Julian relaxed. The tension went from his shoulders, the grip loosened on the grip of the heavy gun, the weight returning to his lower back. He let his jacket cover it.

Relief and frustration were a cocktail of agony for him. He turns suddenly away from them, unable to look at them any longer.

The Snow has slowed. Leaving the road still black and untouched. Only a few flakes fall amidst the rhythmical orange glow of the hazard lights of Julian's car.

He closes his eyes and rubs his hand across his balding scalp. Behind him, he could hear the woman hissing at David, and the scraping of his boots on the roads battered surface.

Julian sighs and speaks, 'I'm fine. Sorry to have bothered you'. And he turns to look at them over his shoulder, smiling as warmly

## *Epithalamium*

and as apologetically as he can, 'Please apologize to your wife for me. I'm sorry if I scared her'

The older man clears his throat, his voice tight. He was indeed tensed and ready. 'That's quite alright. Do you need help?'

Julian smiles again, shakes his head. 'No, I'm okay. I'm just waiting.'

David waits a moment before he replies, the conversation, and the situation at a crossroads. Then he nods and gets silently back into the car.

Julian steps out of the middle of the road, against his own car door and use the roof to support himself.

The other cars engine revs, hot air blasting from the back in a plume of exhaust. It pulls around and moves past Julian. David gives him a curt nod as they pass, the woman's eyes are wide and judgemental and then they are both gone.

Julian has already gotten back into his car by the time they have turned the corner at the end, settling in to wait some more. In the silence, the tortured cries charge from the back of his mind again to torture him.

*Epithalamium*

## 2

There is nothing more satisfying than a cigarette on an evening as cold at this. The heat in your fingers as the end burns away, the enveloping warmth of the smoke as it is drawn down into your lungs. A furnace in your chest, keeping the freezing air at bay.

At least this is how Scarlett, who has never smoked a cigarette in her life, choose to believe it would feel.

She watches the warm, grey cloud unfurl from the mouth of the blonde girl stood away from her. Chloe. She doesn't look cold, even with her cropped leather jacket unzipped, whereas Scarlett was beginning to ache with the effort of trying not to shiver.

It would be about the only thing Scarlett might be envious about.

They stood under the glowing yellow of the vintage street lamp, outside the Golf Clubs main entrance. They were last two on-site after a shift of pulling pints and serving 2-course meals to a function of 38 guests.

Scarlett stamps her flat-soled shoes, wishing she put the thermal tights on that afternoon. She pulls the bobble out of her shocking dyed-red hair so that it falls to her shoulders, around her face, hoping to trap even a little more heat. She has a long face with a square jaw and nose that she has always felt was little too pronounced, a contrast to Chloe's' very soft, round features.

Exhaling another stunning cloud of curling heat, Chloe snatched a sideways glance at Scarlett, a barely concealed sneer. Scarlett stares back but keeps her expression neutral, disinterested. She knows that was the best way to wind her up.

## *Epithalamium*

It was their first shift together after Scarlett had been promoted to Team Supervisor over Chloe, awarding her both a little extra in her pay packet and added authority over the other. Both had stung, perhaps one more than the other. They had never been friends, but they had gotten along well enough. It would be sometime before they would be going out for after-work drinks, if ever. It depended on Chloe alone. Scarlett would be civil. After all, she had won.

A shiver rocks her body, unable to suppress both it and the accompanying groan that bursts from her mouth. Chloe glances over with an arched eyebrow and sucks deeply on her cigarette with apparent deep satisfaction.

Scarlett stamps her feet again and moves from side to side, for a moment giving serious consideration to asking Chloe for a drag. How bad could it be if would warm her just a little?

She is denied the chance to put forth her question as headlights wash over them from the car park entrance. The barrier lifts to allow a vehicle in, it's headlights on full, blinding them both, concealing the car.

Chloe is waiting for a taxi, Scarlett a lift from her boyfriend. They both look hopefully at the advancing car.

\*

Scarlett is pleased to discover that she cannot see her breath anymore. The heater in the cab of the van sees to that. She unwraps the scarf from her neck, glancing in the wing mirror at Chloe. The silhouette of the girl getting smaller in the darkness,

*Epithalamium*

until she is only a little cloud against the Golf Clubs exterior lights.
 Scarlett clicks the seat belt into its slot and looks over at the man beside her in the driving seat. She finds him deeply attractive. Chris has a big, confident jaw blanketed with a mane of dirty blonde, and messy, curly hair to match. He feels her looking, returns the gaze with his own deep grey eyes.
 'Good shift?'
 Scarlett laughs a little, more of a scoff. 'It was okay.'
 'Chloe?'
 'She behaved as expected.'
 Chris chuckles and slows the van at the end of the Golf Clubs drive, waits for a car to pass before moving out to join the stream.
 'She being a cunt?'
 Scarlett frowns. She hates the word. 'Chris, come on.'
 He grins. A boyish grin that disarms her in spite of herself and cannot help but return, 'But yes, she was.'
 'Then I hope you gave her shit', he continues, stopping the van at a set of lights, three cars back, ready to turn right.
 'A bit. Put on cutlery polishing, didn't I?'
 'Good girl.'
 Red turns to amber then green. The cars head pull away, Chris follows onto Derby Road, waits for them to filter into the left lane and guns the engine. He races down the outside just in time to beat the next set of light at the roundabout and flies the transit van around the curve so fiercely that Scarlett has to hold her seat belt to stop her being pressed into her door.
 The van straightens out, the speed picks up, 10 miles an hour

## *Epithalamium*

over the limit. Scarlett doesn't mind. It's been a long day and she too is eager to get home, to the promise of a hot shower, warm pyjamas and a glass of wine. Maybe even a quickie with Chris before loading Netflix and falling asleep to it. A blissful dream made sweeter by its simple attainability.

Chris drops a gear, pushes the gas and the van flies through another questionable amber, swinging left down the ramp onto the ring road.

'Ah, shit' Chris mutters slowing quickly, slipping between a range rover ahead and Corsa behind. Brake lights blind them.

Scarlett cranes her neck to look over the car.

Flashing orange light ahead. The snow has started again, just a little, but enough to make seeing distances difficult.

'What is it?', Scarlett asks.

Chris taps the steering wheel in annoyance, 'Road works. Sunday, isn't it? Bastards always do this shit when they think it's going to be quiet. Fuck this.'

He turns the van sharply, cuts across to the right lane in front of a green Mazda 5 that honks angrily. In another quick movement, he manoeuvrers into a gap in the central reservation. Four cars come towards him, but he throws the van out anyway, forcing them to brake sharply.

Scarlett winces, thrown about but says nothing this time. He's driving like a prat, but she really does want to get home. 'Where are you taking us?'

'Down by Dunkirk. In the industrial estate, there's a road split by bollards, but I can squeeze the van through. I've done it before', he proclaims proudly.

*Epithalamium*

'Just don't get us stopped by the police.'
'It'll be fine, babe.'
Chris does as promised, taking his van back off the ring road and into a housing estate where at the end of a road the route is blocked by a raised curbstones and a row of concrete bollards covered in brightly coloured graffiti. Shifting into first, Chris bumps up onto the pavement on the right and eases the van between the rightmost bollard and the building.

Scarlett cannot help but hold her breath as the panels come within literal inches of the pillar, but Chris succeeds without a scratch. The suspension bounces and creaks as he lurches back onto the road and in a fashion typical of his driving style accelerates aggressively into the dark estate.

Warehouses and factories whiz by Scarlett's window. A right turn leads them onto a long road, gritty with loose, broken tarmac and littered with deep pots holes.

'If she's being a bitch, you should tell your manager', Chris says suddenly. He's clearly been ruminating on it whilst breaking traffic laws.

Scarlett shrugs, 'I will. I want to handle it myself first, but, yeah, I totally will report her to Steve if I need to.'

'As soon as she learns that...', Chris stops and slows the van, 'What's this twat doing?'

Scarlett squints through the falling snow. Heavier now.

Orange lights pulse. Small. Two of them flashing in unison at the side the road. A car; Vauxhall Vectra, dark blue. Beside it is the shape of a man.

As they draw closer, Scarlett sees that he is standing in the middle

*Epithalamium*

of the street, facing away from them.

*

Julian hears the van long before it turns onto the road. Crunching gears and hard revs are a herald to its arrival. He is aware of it gaining speed towards him, the diesel engine roaring, increasing in pitch; third gear, a grind into fourth then quieter. Piercing squeal. Brakes applied.
Slowing.
He knows it is coming to a stop before he turns.
Snow whips about him. He licks his lips. They hurt still. Worse.
The headlights, pale gold this time. Tungsten. Calming. Not the harsh white of newer cars. And angled lower so that he can quite clearly see the driver in the glow from the street lamp.
Male. Bearded. Young, but big.
Julian feels the anxiety build in his stomach. He's really big.
Movement in the passenger seat. His eyes flick over. The urban light illuminates her quite clearly.
Something else rises out of the anxiety, different, an extension of it.
Excitement.
And hope.

*

The van's engine idles, making the cab shudder relentlessly. The rev needle sinks and jumps, dancing to a rhythm only it can hear.

*Epithalamium*

'Is he broken down or something?'. Scarlett asks, unable to break eye contact with the man on the road. His mouth is turned slightly upwards. It's not a smile, not even close, but there is a glimmer of something in the shape of his lips as he licks them.
'Looks like'
Julian is not tall, 5 foot 7 or 8, perhaps and a little round, but not fat. His face to is rounded, with a nose that is narrow at the top and slightly bulbous at the bottom. The unforgiving burnt glow of the streetlamp reflects off a broad pate covered with only the finest of hair, cut short. Most of his hair sits at the back and above his ears. Lank. A little longer than it should be.
Scarlett shifts in her seat. Suddenly uncomfortable. Suddenly too warm. She switches the blowers down, reduces the heat. Still, the man stares at her.
'Chris, I don't like it. I want to go', the words tumble out unexpectedly.
Chris turns his own hazards on, reaches for the door. Scarlett grabs his arm.
'What are you doing?'
'I'm seeing if he's alright. He looks - '
She grips his arm tighter, 'Yeah, I know. He looks creepy. Chris, seriously, I don't like it.'
Ignoring her, Chris opens the door, unclips his belt and steps out with one foot. He calls over the top of his door, 'Mate, you alright?'
Julians' gaze drifts from Scarlet to Chris. His head moves first, turning and his eyes follow after. His mouth opens, but he doesn't answer. There is something forming on his lips, stuck

*Epithalamium*

behind his teeth.

 Scarlett watches as one of his hand twitches. Fingers rub against thumb nervously. Then the hand moves slowly, discreetly, behind his back where it quite clearly grips something out of sight there.

*Epithalamium*

## 3

'Chris... get back inside.'

Her voice gets Julian's attention. His eyes flit back. Chris notices this. He steps out of the van fully, moves to the side of his door.

Julian registers the movement, takes an involuntary step back. Looks at Chris. Easily 6 foot 2 with broad shoulders and steady eyes.

Chris calls over again, his voice louder, deeper, 'To be honest mate, not keen on how you're looking at my missus. Now, is there something I can help you with?'

Julian finds his voice, hoarse though, broken, 'I'm sorry. I'm fine' He exhales, breath unsteady. 'Thank you. Thank you for stopping, but I'm okay now.'

Chris frowns. Julian cannot hold his gaze, keeps looking over at Scarlett. Her eyes are aware of his other hand, the tension in it. 'Chris...'

The hand appears suddenly.

It is empty. Open. Outstretched.

Julian takes a step away, 'I'm okay.'

Chris stares for a moment, then nods curtly and gets back in the van, 'Fucking weirdo. Let's go.' He pushes the handbrake down, revs the engine, turns the wheel. The van the pulls out on a wide arc away from Julian, now stood by his car and quickly races away.

Scarlett watches him through her window they pass by. He is watching her. He doesn't look away. It is only now than Scarlett realizes that her heart is pounding fiercely in her chest and a dead

*Epithalamium*

weight has found its way into her stomach and now sits uncomfortably at the bottom.

Chris' eyes are set on the road ahead, but his mouth has become his typical boyish grin. He reaches over and squeezes her knee, 'What a dickhead, right?'

\*

Twenty minutes later they are pulling up in front of their 3-story terrace in the middle of a quiet new build street. Chris mutters his usual aggravations about Paul, their next-door-but-one neighbour who insists on parking two out of his three cars where ever he feels like it. The result is many cross words between not just Chris and Paul, but Paul and most others. The neighbour, however, fails to see the problem and repeatedly reminds those who accost him on the subject that by law he can park where ever he wants. Despite this, he regularly argues with Chris if Chris decides to park his van in front of Paul's own house. It is a cycle, Scarlett has come to believe, that is doomed to go on forever. Or until one of them no longer lives there.

Fortunately, with it being a little past midnight, there is little chance of Paul seeing Chris squeeze his van between the Alfa Romeo and Volkswagon Passat. The next morning, however, the drawing of Paul kitchen curtains will reveal the transit and the mere inches between it and his precious cars. The sequence will begin again.

Doors slam. The remote lock clicks. Scarlett wrestles keys from her little handbag and they bustle inside, out of the biting cold.

*Epithalamium*

Coats are hung, or dumped on the stairs respectively. Shoes are kicked off or placed neatly on the rack. A beer is cracked, wine is poured. Scarlett vanishes to find her much-anticipated pyjamas.

\*

Chris stands outside the French-doors, looking out at the small but neat garden. A small floodlight illuminates half his face as he blows smoke up into the night air. It clicks off. He waves absently to wake it up again.

It is quiet. Even the usually loud sound of traffic from the bypass behind the nearby crop of trees is only a whisper at this time. He places the cigarette between his lips, sucks, swallows, exhales gratefully. He doesn't smoke at work. Relies solely on the Vape though he finds it very unsatisfying. He allows himself a single cigarette a day, and it is always worth the wait.

There is a pressure on his waist. He looks down to see a pair of hands snaking around his torso, climbing to his chest and pulling him. Scarlett presses herself against him from behind, lets out a contented sigh.

They say nothing for a moment. Content in the quiet and the stillness. An instant between seconds.

'I'll have a word, you know, Scarlett; with your manager, if Chloe's making life hard for you at work.'

Chris feels Scarlett move, ducking under his arm, encircling his waist. She has changed into a lilac pyjama t-shirt with a rabbit on it and blue shorts from another set.

'I know you would', she replies, 'I can deal with it. Honest.'

*Epithalamium*

On her tip toes, she kisses his lips and her eyes fall on his. He knows this look. Until this point, he had decided that he was too tired to shower. A day of ripping out someone's bathroom and dragging the heavy, ageing porcelain down a long alleyway to a skip had taken its toll on him.

That said, he wasn't bothered that his mind has now been changed.

He leans down, kisses her firmly, letting her know that the message had been received, 'I'm going to jump in the shower.'

'Good.' She wraps her arms around his neck, pulls him into a tight hug that includes her hips, before releasing him.

Chris tosses the cigarette, an expertly aimed flick that finds its target two gardens away. He winks at Scarlett and heads inside, climbs the stairs to the bathroom.

He strips off his dust covered work trousers, his plaster and paint-stained fleece, his sweat-infused t-shirt and dumps all on the floor.

The showers knob turns stiffly. The water gushes out, the powerful pressure that he himself had proudly installed. The cascade rattles heavily in the shower tray, the sound filling the tiled room.

Heat adjusted, he steps in. Head under. Water fills his ears. His world is filled with white noise.

\*

Scarlett has her back turned when Julian steps in through the French doors.

## *Epithalamium*

She is stood at the worktop, pouring her second glass of cheap Sauvignon Blanc, ignoring the line set for a legal measure and lets the pale liquid slosh across the lip. The first had gone down effortlessly, far more easily than she'd thought it might. A refill was inevitable.

Raising the glass to her mouth and gulping down, she leans on the counter. The hard white light of the under counter fluorescent bounce back at her from the shiny grey work surface. The shock of the cold wine makes her take a deep breath. The rapid succession of fluid down her throat, crushing the air below forces a belch. She covers her mouth automatically then remembers that Chris is not within earshot. And that powerful shower is running, meaning that she could stand at the bottom of the stairs screaming and he would not hear.

Scarlett opens the cupboard above her head, rummages about in the mess of opened, half-empty packets of biscuits and cakes, searching for inspiration. Nothing. She doesn't want dry.

There are cream cakes in the fridge, she remembers. Jam and fresh cream filled scones from the Morrisons. A pair bought yesterday, but she'd already had one. She stands at the open fridge, tapping her nails on the door.

*Had Chris seen them yet? Would he want the remaining scone? How upset would he be if she has it? He was going to have her later.*
She could risk it.

She takes the scone out of the plastic box, leaving the packaging now empty in the fridge. The door closes. She turns and the shock rocks her body almost painfully. Convulses momentarily. The scone drops to the floor. Wine sloshes from the glass over her hand and the tiled floor.

A gasp. A sharp intake that threatens to burst her lungs. A pulse pounds through her head. She feels like she has been hit with something. She wants to cry. There are no sounds in her.

Julian stands by the breakfast table. One hand rests on it, the other is wrapped around a small handgun.

Scarlett recognizes him immediately. The intense look in his eyes, that unsettling blend of excitement and fear of her.

Julian says nothing. He shifts his grip on the gun in his hand as if trying to get a better hold on it.

The relentless drumming of the shower upstairs on the tray.

Instinct kicks in suddenly for Scarlett. Primal. Irrational. She makes a half step towards the door that leads to the stairs, stopping only when the gun is raised at her. The rational half of her brain takes over. She freezes.

'Don't', Julian's voice is firm. The commanding tone opposes the uncertain look in his eyes.

Uncertain.

Scarlett steps again before her brain can talk her out of it, dashes for the door. She hears the scuffles of feet on the carpet and feels clawed fingers digging into her scalp. Tearing pain that makes tears spring to her eyes. She cries out as she is pulled back, away from the open door and back into the kitchen area.

The shower still hammers away above her head, and she cries out again, louder. She is shoved. Her knee collides with the low cupboard door. The grip tightens on her hair and her hands fly up automatically to try to ease the pressure. The wine glass drops. Smashes loudly.

## *Epithalamium*

She is pushed over the worktop, head pushes down so that it is almost wedged between the pasta jars and the toaster. Breath wafts over her, hot air in her ear, 'Please. Please don't.'

She is confused. Those are the words she was about to utter. She braces herself for whatever happens next, but nothing does.

There is only Julian's heavy respiration. Slow. Shaky. Then he speaks again, a tremble in his voice, 'I need you to - .'

The thundering of falling water above their heads stops.

Nothing.

Footsteps. Wet. Bare. Walking across the landing to the bedroom.

A tug on Scarlett's hair as she is turned forcefully to face him. The grip intensifies as her hair is then pulled, making her bend awkwardly backward over the surface.

The gun is there suddenly. It now appears huge. Terrifying. It's so close to her eyes that she can't focus on it. It vanishes from her vision. But she can smell the metal.

Julian is staring at her intently, his eyes flicking from one of hers to the other and back. He is choosing his words.

Movement upstairs. A drawer opening then slamming shut. Then walking. Walking to the stairs.

Julian leans close to her. His lips are cracked, almost raw and his eyes look red and sore, his cheeks pockmarked from teenage acne. He whispers, 'Make him go away. Make him go away or I will shoot him. I will shoot him and I will kill him. Do you understand?'

Scarlett's fear-dried mouth opens to reply, but only a sob exits.

'Do you understand? I will kill him!' A hoarse threat, a growl.

*Epithalamium*

Chris' bare feet are now descending the stairs.

'I... yes...' she can't manage anymore.

Julian drags her from her painful position on the counter and thrusts her at the door. The door that connects the kitchen-dining room and the porch where the stairs drop into. Julians' hand releases her hair, falls to the back of her collar. The muzzle of the gun is pressed into her spine.

Chris' great bulk appears in the porch. He is surprised to see her standing there, leaning around the open door, looking at him. He stops.

'You shit me up, Scarlett', he says, 'What's up with you?'

'Nothing, babe'

'You been crying or something?'

Scarlett wipes her eyes. They are wet. Her mascara smudges. The gun digs into her back. It hurts.

'I've just been sneezing', she says quickly, with no idea where that lie sprang from, and continues, 'I'll be up a minute.'

'Fine, but I wanted another beer.'

Chris makes to step past her, but she puts her small hand on his big chest, 'I'll bring you one. Go back up. I'll be there.'

Scarlett feels her voice almost breaking. Julian must have too as the pressure in her back increases.

Chris grins. Scarlett loves than smile; he is such a masculine person, almost to the point of cliché and that perpetual clinging to his innate maleness in most areas of his life can be exhausting for her. But in those moments, where he lets go of masculine posturing, constantly needing to be perceived as a man, and that innocent, mischievous smile that must have melted his mother's heart appears; those are the moments when Scarlett knows that she loves him.

Chris looks down at her, grinning, 'What going on?'

Scarlett shakes her head and reaches up, pulls his t-shirt and presses her lips into his. He kisses her back and she longs to tell him that there is a man in their house. That he is threatening to kill him. That he has hurt her. Chris is big. He's had a rough upbringing, been in plenty of fights. She's watched him punch someone for simply hugging her uninvited. Hated him for it. For leaping into violence so unnecessarily.

He could do it now though. He could punch *this* guy. He could win easily. Her attacker was short, clearly not used to what he was now doing. Scarlett knew Chris had done far more in his past than he had admitted to her.

She could tell him now. Whisper it. In seconds this man would be choking on his own blood.

*Epithalamium*

## 4

Tension suddenly in her throat as her collar is pulled, a small but firm gesture. The gun pushed so far into her back it was starting really hurt.

The gun. Could Chris react faster than the man could pull the trigger? What if he wasn't? What if he was shot and the man still did to her whatever it was he was planning? Her fate would be decided in that moment and Chris would be dead.

Scarlett brakes the kiss and somehow manages to swallow the terrified lump that was rising in her throat, threatening to tell Chris everything.

She presses her forehead against his cheek and whispers, 'Go upstairs, babe. I'll come to you.'

Chris doesn't move for a long moment and Scarlett fears that he might suspect that something is genuinely up. But he doesn't. Instead, he shrugs, kisses her on the head and pounds his way back up the stairs without a second look back.

When he is out of sight and earshot, Scarlett lets the sob out. A long and deep exhalation of despair.

Julian yanks her again, out into the center of the room, peering nervously around the door to make sure Chris has definitely gone.

Satisfied, he breathes out through pursed lips and looks at Scarlets' sorrowful face, 'We're leaving.'

\*

They depart through the French doors. Julian, his hand still

*Epithalamium*

firmly on her pyjama collar, steers her down the path to the small gardens rear gate. The floodlight comes on.

'Open it', he commands and she obeys without a word. Tears are falling from her eyes now, springing hot, turning cold in the winter air. She is pushed out into the narrow alley that runs behind the houses and left, down a set of steps. The freezing concrete slabs hurt her bare feet. Her toes catch on the edges of sharp pebbles.

She thinks of Chris sitting in the warmth of their first-floor living room. Waiting for his beer. Waiting for her. How long will he wait before calling out for her? Before getting annoyed and heading back downstairs to find an open door and no sign of her? What will he do then? Go in the garden, call her mobile? How long until he calls the police? Would he even do that? Chris hates the police; he has never had a good relationship with the law, even when on the theoretical 'right side' of it. Surely he would eventually, when Scarlett didn't answer the call of her name or he realized her phone was ringing where she left it on charge by the bed. Twenty minutes? An hour?

'Scarlett?'

Hope flooded her heart. Her name being called from somewhere behind them, echoing down the alleyway to her and her captor.

'Scarlett, is that you?', the voice follows them. Padding footsteps, slapping on the concrete. Slippers. Chris doesn't wear slippers. 'Who are you with? Stop! Don't you dare ignore me.'

It's Paul, their neighbour, and street-parking rival. She risks a glance back as Julian pushes her on, increasing the speed along the narrow urban ravine. Dressed in a striped dressing gown, he is

## *Epithalamium*

following them with conceited urgency. His voice is nasal and filled with self-importance, 'Who's that with you? Where are you going at this hour?'

Scarlett looks at Julian. His eyes are wide, burning with frustration.

Paul does not stop, 'Excuse me! Stop right now. I have had a look at the front and you can tell that boyfriend of yours that I do not find his parking the least bit amusing!'

They all descend another set of steps. It takes them deeper behind the houses. The walls of the garden now rise above them on both sides, 8 feet or more. The sound of Paul's relentless badgering echoes back at them but kept within the steep brick barricades.

Julian keeps shoving Scarlett on. Ahead it appears like a dead end, but it is an illusion. In truth, it is a T-junction; to the left access to several more houses, to the right an exit to the main road.

'Scarlett; you and your friend are being very rude!'

They reach the junction. Julian stop and turns, 'Go away!'

Paul is taken aback by at first, but his arrogance quickly reaffirms control over the conversation, 'Do not speak to me like that. Where is Chris? I want to - '

Julian turns and steers Scarlett around the corner. Ahead there is the light from the main road. Parked at the mouth of the alley is a car. Dark blue Vectra. The same car from the roadside, Scarlett cannot help but notice.

'I must say, Scarlett, your taste in men has gotten worse! This behaviour is truly nothing short of disgusting!' Paul's voice is

## Epithalamium

louder, more nasal. It gets worse the angrier he gets. At a certain point, he becomes nails on a chalkboard to Scarlett. She cannot stand that vile little snot. There are times she has daydreamed about hitting him. Or running him down with her car whilst he's still balling at her. That would show him that he can't go around throwing his weight about. Right now she's terrified of what is happening to her, and he's having a tantrum about Chris parking too close to his cars! It's he who's disgusting! It's he who deserves to have this happen to him!

Then Paul pushes it too far. He reaches out, grabs Julian arm and tries to turn him. Scarlett can see Julian is already on the edge of his sanity. He is spun around, eyes wide and angry, spittle forming around his cracked mouth, the hand with the gun rises.

Paul does not see it immediately. He cannot see it. It is so unexpected that it simply cannot exist in his reality. When it does, a pathetic sob escapes his mouth and he steps away. He hands clutch at the walls either side.

The flash lights up the alley for an instant. The crack is like the sky splitting. It hurts Scarlett's ears so much she covers them.

*Epithalamium*

## 5

Paul has not moved.

Scarlett has never seen anyone shot except in films. There they either cry out, clutch their chest and fall gracefully to the floor, or they fly backward, several feet or more.

Paul just stands there for a moment. It's like the pain take a few seconds to register, It's like his brain is arguing with itself. It has observed and acknowledged the existence of the gun. Witnesses the pulling of the trigger, the flash, and the sound. It's felt the impact of the projectile. The smashing inward of his chest plate, the sharp fragments of bone ripping through his lungs and heart.

And yet for a moment, it refuses to believe it. *It's a mistake. This can't happen. Not to him. He's just a normal guy. He doesn't deserve something like this. This isn't fair.*

The lack of belief on his face is still there as blood starts pumping out of the darkening patch on his chest. He doesn't touch it. His hands wave about like they're grasping for something or someone. His legs go weak before he knows what's happening. Paul starts to lower, slowly, like he's deflating.

It's then that the pain clearly starts to register. A natural hit of adrenaline can only so so much when your the contents of your chest cavity is pouring out. His mouth opens. No sound. His lungs are collapsing. His traumatized heart is going into arrest.

The only sound comes from Julian who lets out an anguished cry and grabs Scarlett's hair again. He forces her to break into a stumbling run towards the waiting car.

She looks back. Paul is on the floor now, in the shadows. His are

waving. Reaching out. Like a baby, crying and desperate for its mothers embrace. Alongside her fear, for herself, she feels something else. Another emotion that clings to her like a detestable vestigial twin. Always there, only now making itself known.
*Relief.*
It's a tiny speck of hope floating in the choking darkness of her predicament. Surely someone had heard the gunshot. They'll come out to investigate. They'll see her being taken away at gunpoint. They'll call the police. They'll tell Chris.
Paul being shot was the best possible thing to have happened to her.
*She was glad he was shot.*
*Glad it was him.*
*Glad.*
She felt nauseated at the realization of her feelings. Felt it rising in her chest. She might have vomited if Julian had not thrown her against the door of the car.
She takes a gasp of air, swallowing nausea, for the first time taking pleasure in the cold air.
Julian too takes in big, greedy lungfuls. His left hand is still gripping her hair tightly, the right is resting the weight of the gun between her shoulder blades.
He is shaking violently. She can feel it on her back. He is shaken upon. Maybe even scared. Maybe more scared than her.
A tiny wave of courage washes over her and, crushed against the door of the strange car by a violent man, she finds her voice, 'Please don't do this.'

*Epithalamium*

Her scalp is suddenly on fire. Julian yanks her away from the car and screams in her ear, 'Shut up!' It is pure venom; as if she has committed some horrendous sin against him. She cowers, her lower lip trembling. He is looking at her. Through her, thinking.

Julian leans down past her and heaves the front passenger door open, pushes her inside. Instinct makes her resist for a second. She grabs the sides of the car, tenses her arms, but he slams his fist into her biceps and she falters.

Into the seat, she longs for a second to gather her thoughts, to look for options, but she is being shoved again. Hard, hands against her shoulders, her neck, her face.

'Move! Move over!'

Then he is forcing himself inside, into the same seat. Pushing her, hitting her arm and shoulder with flat hands until she manages to somehow place her backside in the driver's seat. He sits where she was a moment ago, pull the door shut, but now he has trapped her legs under his.

He lets out a scream of frustration, grabbing at her bare legs, pulling them up, pushing them away. Her shins scrap cross the sharp dials of the centre console, the gear lever digs into her calves until finally, she is on her own side.

No moment of respite. Julian reaches over suddenly, making her jump, lift her hands defensively. A rattle and click. He has inserted keys into the ignition. A cough. Rumble. The engines explode into life and then there is the gun again. Pointing at her.

Julian has shoved himself into the car, as far away from Scarlett as he can in the tight space. His eyes are discs of white in the dark interior. The gun shakes so much Scarlett is terrified that he will

## *Epithalamium*

fire it accidentally.

He swallows and takes a long breath before he speaks, 'You will drive. Okay? You will drive where I tell you to. Or I will shoot you. I will shoot you and it will *hurt you*. Do you understand what I am saying?'

For the first time, she notices how well he speaks. He has a local accent, Midlands for sure, but his elocution betrays more than a comprehensive school education. He talks slowly to her because he doesn't want to be misunderstood. He wants her to do as he has asked. Paul did not.

Scarlett nods and places her own shaking hands on the steering wheel and whispers, 'Where?'

'I don't know', he stammers, looking around the car, 'Just... just start driving. I'll tell you when and where to turn.'

\*

There are few things in life that provide so much sheer pleasure at scrolling down the endless lists on Netflix. It is perhaps one of Scarlett most favourite things in her life, and although she fully understands the mundane and potentially shallow nature it, she also cannot her bring her self to care. The rhythmic clicking on her remote as the explores, one title at a time, watching the trailers, judging it and adding it to her ever-expanding to-watch list. And sat on her expensive, comfortable sofa. Her central heating keeping the living room at a lazy 26 degrees Celsius. A glass of wine in her free hand. Her feet resting idly on the lap of the man she adores.

## *Epithalamium*

*This is what she should be doing right now.*

Not driving aimlessly down a long rural road, barely dressed, with a gun pointed at her by an unhinged stranger.

The thought of this, the unfairness of it, makes her gasp. It's not a sob. She feels that she's used all that up. It's like something rising it her chest and makes her take an involuntary inward breath. She cannot help it. Her mind wants to cry, but her body won't let her.

The road is dark. The streetlamps left a mile behind as they left the newly built housing estates on the edge of Hucknall. In this darkness, Scarlett cannot see Julian beside her, and he says nothing to her. For a little while, she pretends that she is alone and that she is simply driving home. To Chris. To the little corner of heaven that she has rented.

There is a sharp right-hand bend and the street-lamps are back. Light washes the shadows from Julian. Scarlett slows the car as the road bends left again. There is a mini roundabout at the bottom.

'Left', mutters Julian, his forehead pressed against the cold window.

Wordlessly, Scarlett does as commanded. They are on Watnall Road. She knows it well, having used this road when she drives herself to work. Chris insists the ring-road is quicker, but Scarlett has always preferred the quieter A6002 that slips courteously behind Billborough and Wollaton.

Time passes slowly as Julian directs her. Left at Nottingham Road, straight across at the Nuthall junction. Keep left. Keep going.

Silence when Julian is not telling her where to go. It gives Scarlett

*Epithalamium*

time to gather her thought, to check her emotions, to try to soothe her frayed nerves. She is someone who is generally guilty of panicking, of knee-jerk reactions. With this time to think, she tells herself that although this is a situation where panicking is quite acceptable, it is probably the worst thing that she can do.

She looks over at Julian. The gun is still trained on her but is resting on his thigh. His eyes are closed, his lips moving, saying something she cannot hear.

Julian moves suddenly, startling her, reaches into his inside jacket pocket and pulls out a small, cheap mobile phone. He taps a button, illuminating the screen but sighs deeply and lets it drop into his lap.

Another sigh. He taps his head on the window, licking those dry, cracked lips.

Scarlett gulps down her fear, and speaks, 'What do you want?'

Julian looks over at her suddenly, incredulously, fury in his eyes. The gun on his leg twitches. 'No. Don't talk. Drive. Just drive.'

Scarlett looks away, back to the road. Green lights ahead. The A610 crosses the ring-road. They're heading into the city. She prays for a police car; but what would she do then? Shout? Wave? Flash her headlights? She'd have a bullet in her before the police car had even turned around.

Or would she? So far her kidnapper has seemed unwilling to kill her. He had threatened to kill Chris, not her. He had said that he would hurt her, not kill her. She couldn't be sure that she wasn't misremembering these frantic conversations and yet there was hope. If he didn't want to kill her, and least just now, then there was hope.

*Epithalamium*

The flew over the humpback bridge of Bobbersmill. There were red lights ahead.

'Go left', Julian mumbles, rubbing his head, 'No, straight ahead. Go straight.'

Scarlett position the car in the center lane, brakes for the reds and mutters, her voice small, 'If you tell me where we're going, it'd be easier.'

'Easier!' Julian spits the word, laughing venomously, 'Do I look as if I care about easier? Nothing about this night has been easy!'

His laugh cracks. A sob hid within. His finger turns into claws. They scratch at his head, his face.

Scarlett exhales, calming herself, trying to keep her voice level, 'What I mean is I might know a better way - '

Julians laugh is high pitched. Spittle flies from his mouths. He shakes his head at her, his eyes suggest that she has just said something outrageous. Stupid. 'A better way? Are you serious? A better way. Do you mean quicker? You want to get there quicker? I.. I don't - .'

He is moving around in his seat. Looking around with jerky, almost bird-like movements.

Something registers in Scarlett's brain. Something important, but it remains in darkness. She frowns, feeling like she needs to keep talking, 'Please tell why you're doing this. Please, I'm scared. I just want to go home.'

Truth in every word. That pressure in her chest again, her mind wanting to cry and plead again. No. Control it. Julian is shaking his head, looking out of the window.

Scarlett keeps going, 'Do you know me?'

*Epithalamium*

Julian snorts derisively.

'Do I know you?'

Head shaking, a mocking expression.

'Then why me?' To her horror, Scarlett realizes that she has raised her voice. Angry and indignant. Julian's head snaps to her and he leans over, almost between her and the wind-shield. now practically facing the wrong way in the car.

*That feeling again. There is something. Inching into the light, but still out of reach.*

'No', Julian replies, his voice thick with condescension, 'We don't know each other. We've never met. You don't know me and I certainly do not know someone like you.'

He rests his tongue between his teeth thoughtfully. The wet muscle waving up and down obscenely before shooting out dragging itself across the lips. 'I had to choose. That was all. I had to choose and I chose you.'

He looks deep into her face, but when her eyes flick from the road to meet his, they dart away. Julian throws himself back into the seat. He smashes his elbow into the car door, a second time, a third. Screaming as he does.

'I chose you!' Then he laughs again, shaking his head, 'Though not at first of course. I couldn't. I couldn't do it. I couldn't choose. It was impossible! How the hell am I meant to do that? Where the hell do you start with something like that? Huh?'

The car is now climbing the hill between Lenton and Hyson Green. Scarlett looks over at Julian; he is so low in his seat. His knee tucked up high, one foot resting on the dashboard.

*There it is again. What is she seeing and not seeing?*

*Epithalamium*

'I drove around at first, with my headlights off. I'd read somewhere that there were these people who drive around at night with no headlights on, and when people flashed them, they would turn around, give chase and pull them over... attack them', Julian explains without a breath, 'So I did, and people kept flashing me, but I couldn't do it. I mean I turned the car around once, followed them all the way to a set of lights but... I don't know...'

Scarlett stops the car. A red cast falls across them. The gun on Julian's lap twitches. Crimson light reflects off its metal body. He continues, a staccato of words, like he can't stop now, 'So I pulled over, put on my hazards, you know, so I wouldn't get run into on that dark road... and someone stopped to see if I need help. It was a girl, a woman... a little older than me but really pretty. She had dark hair, sort of curvy without being fat. It seemed right...'

He trails off, looks as if he might vomit. The red light remains. They are caught between cycles.

Julian starts again, 'But there was a little boy... on the seat beside her, and another in the back. Good god... I couldn't... I couldn't... but then there was an old man and it looked like he had a girl next to him.'

He laughs, rolls his eyes, 'It wasn't a girl. She was old. Really old. Oh, god...' Julian sits forward, repeating the phrase, leans over his knees, over the gun, clutching his stomach.

It hits her like a bolt of lightning and a wave of excitement and anxiety emerges in her chest.

*He is not wearing his seatbelt.*

Julian peers over at her, and he looks away from the empty slot by his hip. 'Then you came by I nearly cried. You were perfect. You were exactly what I needed. And for that... I am sorry.'

Scarlett frowns at that. The lights turn green. She eases up the clutch, presses the gas and brings it up to speed as they reach the top of the hill and begin to downward slope into the city.

*She's perfect? For what? He's sorry? The seatbelt? He's not wearing it!* So many questions so quickly. Her head began to spin. She could only think of one thing at a time.

The seat belt. Why was her mind telling her it was important?

Julian was still staring at her. There was pain in his face now. Sympathy. Guilt, perhaps.

*No seatbelt.*

Then the idea formed in her mind. It has been there all along, but she was so wrapped up in her misery that it could not crystallize.

Now it had.

It was clear.

It was insane.

*Dangerous*

She couldn't do it. *Couldn't*.

Her body disagreed. Before she knew, her foot was pressing the gas gently. The needle of the speedometer crept up to 28 and 30 and 32.

Julian gave her a strange smile, 'What a night. What a bloody awful night.' and he buried his face in his hands, the gun now right by his face, looking straight at her hers.

A little more gas, slowly, gently. Keep the gears high so the engine pitch doesn't change too suddenly.

*Epithalamium*

*28.*

*33.*

There are no other cars. At 45mph on an inner city street, it seems very fast.

Julian is still mumbling into his hand, eyes obscured.

Scarlett's breath becomes shaky. This is so stupid. He'll realize what she's doing and he'll shoot her. She should stop.

She doesn't.

*35.*

*38.*

Julian sits back suddenly, pushes himself back into his seat's headrest, 'Do you know how I knew it had to be you?'

*40.*

Scarlett lets out a gasp. She can't help it. The adrenaline is starting to make her leg shake. She involuntarily pushes the gas harder. The engine rev. loud.

*43.*

*44.*

Julian stops his monologue and looks out of the window. Suddenly aware of the speed. Feels exposed. Grabs the empty slot for his belt. His eyes widen.

Scarlett's closes her eyes. Shifts her foot from the gas.

Crushes the brake with everything she has.

*Epithalamium*

## 6

Julian has never felt such force. That said, it is not something that he is completely aware as it actually happens. The shock of the sudden and brutal change in inertia is such that, at least in atomic terms, it has long since happened before he is able to even remotely grasp the reality of it.

He is thrown from the back of his seat and covers the approximate distance of 2 feet at 44 miles per hour. This means his head completes its journey from its original position to the dashboard in less than a tenth of a second. Had his head not been turned to face Scarlett, he would have been killed outright. As it happens, it is his cheekbone that impacts the hard plastic, shattering the bones and splitting the skin open. His skull, heavier than his brain, moves first, causing the soft matter to be squashed momentarily against the back wall of his cranium. Blood vessel burst, and bruising begins.

Julian knows none of this. He knows the look in Scarlett's eyes before she presses the brake. He knows he has not put his belt on. And he knows that the side of his face has exploded into agony.

It's like he wakes up. Only a second has passed, but it feels as if he's been asleep for hours. The car is stationary. His cheek is on fire. His vision swims and it hurts to move his head or even his eyes. There is a deafening hum in his ears.

Movement. His bloodshot eye swivels. She is grabbing at the door, trying to find the handle. She finds it.

Panic grips him. God no! Please, please no! He reaches out to her, but he is uncoordinated, his hands don't go where he wants

*Epithalamium*

them to.

A click. The door unlocks, opens a crack.

He lunges, crying out with a voice that he has never heard before. His fingers catch her top, then grip the material. She screams and pulls away, pushes the door with her hands, kicking out with her bare feet.

Julian tries to grab with the other hand. He has no fingers. Confusion. Then he understands why.

The gun is in that hand.

*The gun.*

Scarlett sees it, screams, kicks hard. Her heel catches his nose, stunning him. More pain. So much more pain. He yanks on her top, but the extra momentum is his undoing. He loses friction, the fabric slips from his grasp.

He watches her topple out of the open door away from him.

No! He sees everything coming undone. This cannot happen! She doesn't understand what she's doing!

He raises the gun, finger finding the trigger. Shoot her. Make her stop. He's not a marksman, nothing of the sort. With her moving and he barely able to see, he'd just as easily kill than wound her, assuming he hit her at all.

Then the girl is on her feet, galloping away. His head is pounding.

Julian pushes his way out of the other door but falls as soon as his feet touch the ground. He falls against the car but is able to keep himself from crashing into the tarmac. Over the top of the roof, the girl is stumbling away, across the road. He looks around at the wide space around him; roads, painted lanes. Tall buildings

*Epithalamium*

ahead, smaller ones behind, on a misshapen island. There was pubs, all dark and closed; Ropewalk, Sir John Borlase Warren. A long blue building with a clock.

Canning Circus.

He uses his hand on the roof to propel himself around the car, ready to give chase but she is already so far away and he can barely keep his balance.

His hand falls on the open driver door. He gets in, turns the key. It won't move. For a second, his swirling brain can't comprehend why. Then he understands. Julian turns the key all the way off, then rotates it back.

The engine splutters immediately into life, but the car lurches violently and stalls.

Julian cries out with frustration. Scarlett is now across the road, heading into another street, between buildings. Talbot street.

He looks wildly around the car. Why won't it start?

The gear lever sits mockingly in first.

The solving of the mystery seems to settle his mind a little. His eyes focus a bit.

Clutch down. Into neutral, start the ignition, back into first.

Hope once again floods his heart. Looks over. Scarlett disappears between buildings.

Julian guns the engine and turns the car.

\*

Scarlett runs like she hasn't since secondary school, and even then it was under duress. She had never been athletic, or

## *Epithalamium*

particularly physical beyond alcohol-fuelled dancing sessions at Liberty's or Squares. And even then, any calories burnt were immediately replaced by questionable inner city kebabs.

Those days seem such a long time ago. Tumbling uncontrollably towards age 30, it is rare that she is able to go out like she used to. Both her's and Chris' work keep them both busy, usually at opposing hours so that their time together is their time together. Evenings out drinking usually end around midnight, and on those sessions where their younger friends convince them to stay out until the clubs close, she regrets it deeply for days to come. She used to love clubs. Even more, since she met Chris. Her first memory of him was his big hand closing around her hips from behind. Already fending of several grotesque and unsolicited male advances that evening, she had turned to tell him to fuck off but had walked heart-first into the damned grin of his.

A sob rose from her chest, making her gasp as her bare feet slammed repeatedly against the rough pavement.

Chris. She needed to get back to him. Where was she?

She'd barely registered where she was driving when Julian was beside her, let alone where it was that she'd carried out her escape plan. Looking around she could see only tall buildings, a long brick wall on her left. To her right a road jutted off, buildings mostly covered in steel scaffolding. They looked dark. Safe.

She turns sharply, almost tripping on the curbstone and sprinting to the metal haven. Grabbing for a pole, she stopped her self. A car's headlight washed over for a second and pushes herself back against the wall. A dark car goes past, down the road, she was going to go down. She couldn't tell if it was a Vectra.

*Epithalamium*

Scarlett freezes for a second, trying to get her bearings. Was this Wollaton Steet? It looked like it might be. A gust blew over her, suddenly reminding her of the icy weather and the lack of warm clothes on her. She needed to move. The city centre was down the hill, she remembered this much. There would be people there. Help. Maybe someone would lend a phone, to call Chris. Then he could come and get her.

She shivers. The warmth was leaving her body rapidly. Move.

Scarlett shoves herself away from the wall and hurries down the hill, keeping under the shelter of the scaffolding until it runs out after a hundred yards.

Her hand on the wall reassuringly, Scarlett keeps going, feeling exposed now. She looks backward, as well as ahead. Looking for Julian, searching for a face. Any face.

There is no one.

*How could there be no one?*

Because it was probably nearly 1.30 in the morning on a Sunday night in winter.

Headlights throw her shadow out in front of her, and she stopped running and flattened herself against the wall, her heart in her throat. White light in her eyes.

The car slows and Scarlett makes ready to run again. The glare fades. It is a white Skoda. There are signs on the doors. A light on top. A taxi.

The driver looks at her, at her terrified face that changes suddenly into hope. She steps towards him. He looked at her attire then accelerates away.

'Please!', she calls after the car as it speeds away down the street,

*Epithalamium*

padding along after it. Her feet are starting to go numb, her toes sore from hitting the concrete.

There is a set of traffic lights ahead. They turn to red long before the taxi gets to it, so it has no choice but to stop. Scarlett breaks for it, ignoring the increasing pain in her feet as she draws closer. She knows the driver is just looking for an easy fair, don't want hassle or drama or a crazy-looking girl dressed in bedclothes. But she needs help. She knows that she can convince him as soon as he understands that she is not crazy or drunk.

The traffic going the other way starts to move. Scarlett steps out into the road to cross towards her target. An angry honk from another car coming down, admonishing her before stopping beside the taxi.

Breathing hard, she gets closer. Crossing traffic passing the nose of the taxi.

She stops suddenly, crying out. A dark blue Vectra. It stops as soon as she sees it, the window comes down. Julian stares back at her.

\*

The girl is staring at Julian in horror and disbelief, stood behind a taxi and another car both waiting at the lights. Her eyes go from him to the taxi, to him again.

*She's going for the taxi.*

A horn from the car behind him, wanting him to move from the middle of the junction. Julian's mind, still fuzzy from the concussion, cannot process a course of action.

## *Epithalamium*

Another beep. Long. Too long.

Scarlett takes a step towards the taxi. He looks at her. She stops, then starts again.

Julian revs the engine, turns the wheel sharply to the right. The road that Scarlett's is on is One-Way, 2 lanes and are blocked by the taxi and another car facing him. He noses aggressively towards it, honks his horn, trying to get the car move so that he can squeeze around it. Bump the curve. Go up the one-way street.

Scarlett loses her nerve, starts to running back up the street again, away from him.

A horn from behind Julian, from the car he is blocking. Horns from him. The lights change to green for the taxi and the other car, horns blaring from them.

Julian revs, advances. The car replies with its honking, annoyed waving from within.

The girl is almost out of sight behind the cars.

Julian yells and turns the wheel again, taking the car along the route intended by law but at a speed deemed dangerous. He ploughs out of the next junction, onto Derby Road and accelerates rapidly. All he can do it go around again, an illegal right at Canning Circus, then right again back down Wollaton to intercept her.

She won't know.

He can do this.

\*

Scarlett's looks behind her as all the car at the junction starting

*Epithalamium*

beeping at each other. The Vectra roars away, the car following it goes and the taxi and its partner drive on.

Alone again.

She keeps running for a second, then stops, holding onto the wall, concentrates her mind. That guy went straight ahead, which means he'll hit Derby Road, which is one way. He can only turn right.

Scarlett grabs her hair, pulling it, trying to think. That would take him back to where she stopped the car. He can't turn right there, he'd have to go straight on.

No. He was trying to come up this road. A one-way. He doesn't care.

Scarlett starts moving, back down the hill as fast as she can, back to the junction.

There are no cars there now. Not a single one.

The sound of a car carries on the wind, a squeal of tyres.

At the top of the hill, a car is turning aggressively. She can't tell its colour, but the sound of it betrays a car being thrashed in too low a gear.

Scarlett turns right along Vernon, sprints as fast her legs and burning feet can take her. She hits the main road. Four lanes wide, grid-locked at least twice a day. Now, nothing.

An engine behind it. It might not even be him, but she cannot risk it. Not even the time it would take to look behind.

Across the road is a Catholic church, beside it a road, dark and unlit. She runs for it, dashes between a few green bollards, onto smooth cobblestone that makes her gasp. They are even colder than the tarmac.

## *Epithalamium*

A shriek of tyres breaking. She risks a glance. The Vectra has stopped at the junction to let a lorry by but is quickly leaping out, across the four lanes to her.

Scarlett barrels on, down the road until she realized it is anything but. A wall at the end. Taller than her, smooth drystone. Behind her the Vectra bumps up, between the chained-bollards, into what is clearly a car park for the church.

She looks around. *No! This cannot be it.*

There is a small car parked by the wall. An old red Nissan Micra.

Scarlett takes a quick look at the Vectra that as now stopped, the driver's door opening and makes her choice. She throws herself up onto the bonnet. The metal is so cold it burns her skin. She slips, denting the thin metal.

She hears Julian shouting at her but heaves herself up onto the roof. The wall is only a foot away, but there is still 2 feet of vertical. She'll never lift her leg that high.

A bang as Julian slams against the Micra. A hand brushing her foot.

Scarlett leaps. She fires her legs as hard as she can, arms outstretched. Her stomach lands hard on the top of the wall with, winding her. Squirming, she overbalances, the weight of her arms tipping her head first into the dark foliage beyond.

*Epithalamium*

## 7

His hand touches her foot, but he cannot make enough contact to grip and she slips away from him. The girl's legs kick high in the air, rattling the tall fir trees. Then they are gone, sucked down, out of sight.

Julian lets out a growl and claws at his head. He is about to heave himself up onto the car when a sound floats towards him; a noise he had longed to hear earlier, but now, in this moment, dreads.

Quickly, he shoves his hand into his jacket pocket and takes out the basic mobile phone. It shrieks at him with a high pitched polyphonic tone. The screen displays the words Private Number.

Julian stares at it for a moment, then at the wall. He cannot hear movement from the other side.

Seven rings and it stops. The silence is worse than the ringing.

It starts again.

Damn it. He can't ignore it. He has to answer. But what can he say? Excuses won't be tolerated. He can't answer it, there are no suitable answers to give. He'll only make it worse. Pretend he didn't hear it.

He clutches his chest as it tightens with fear. What if it makes it worse?

It stops ringing again and remains silent.

Julian holds it in his hand, not moving.

It's not going to ring again. Not right now. He has time to make it right.

Without another thought, he pulls himself painfully up onto the bonnet of the small car, then onto the roof. The panel depresses

## *Epithalamium*

deeply under his weight, making dull, clanging noises. He leans over and grips the rough stone of the wall and half jumps, half pulls. His shin crashes into the rock, making him cry out, and his weigh threatens to unbalance him, pulling him back the way he has just come.

Leaning forward, shifting and scraping his knees along the wall he is able to redistribute his centre of gravity ahead, and with a little shuffle leaps away.

Julian clears the undergrowth, landing hard, falling to his knees and elbows on the hard, frozen lawn. His hands slap on the stiff soil, his kneecaps too. His head jars with the impact, making his already agonizing headaches worse.

He forces himself to his feet and looks around. There is a path ahead of him, leading into the dark reaches of this garden. To his left a metal gate, half open. Hurrying through it, he sees there is the well-trimmed garden behind the church. The sort of area designed for photographs after a wedding service inside.

Julian breaks into the best run he can with his stiff, sore knees. Along a gravel path, towards a round building with a pitched roof and through another car park.

Movement ahead hurried to scuffling noise on his right, then a silhouette dashing along in front of the metal railings towards the barrier. Julian sprints, moving to intercept her before she reaches the exit. A girlish cry as he grabs for her.

\*

Scarlett lets out a long breath, and draws in an even longer one.

*Epithalamium*

Or at least tries. She finds she can only inhale a little before the pain makes her blow it all back out again.

Lying on her back on the bushes behind the wall, winded, bruised and scratched from the twisted branches of the fir trees, she cannot move.

She is helpless. When he follows her over the wall, which he will any second now, he'll land right on top of her. Then despite her desperate efforts, she'll be right back in his car being taken to whatever fate he has in mind for her.

A crash and a moan.

He has landed.

But there is no rustling of bushes or movement of the foliage around her.

Although it hurts, Scarlett moves her head to look out between the branches and evergreen at the neat grass beyond. Julian is there, on all fours, groaning and lifting himself up.

He overshot her. Leapt over the bushes, instead of falling uncontrollably head first into them like she did. There was something to be said for a lack of physical prowess after all.

Now not daring to move, she watches as he looks around, he heads off away from her, through an open gate, out of sight. She hears him crunching down a path.

She starts counting in her head. When she gets to forty-six, she hears sudden running and a shocked cry. Female, then male. Julian is apologizing, angry shouting from the apparent couple. The voices fade.

Scarlett forces herself to take her count to 150 before she takes a deep breath, sits up and starts to pull herself out of the shrubbery.

*Epithalamium*

The lawn is painfully hard and cold under her bare knees. Once in the open, she stops and listens carefully.

Nothing.

Scarlett is about to stand up when something catches her eye. Something dark and solid, but small and alien against the lighter grass.

She puts her hand on it, picks it up.

A mobile phone. Alcatel. A very basic model. Like the one her kidnapper had in the car. He must have dropped it when he jumped over the wall.

Scarlett smiles as he cradles the little bundle of hope in her hand. She presses buttons until the screen lights up, showing a half-full battery.

*She can call Chris.*

Her hands shaking with excitement, he starts to dial his number. The buttons are stiff and badly made, so she presses the wrong digits several times until the screen is filled with the 11 numbers that spell her deliverance.

She presses *Call*.

Immediately the screen changes and her heart sinks.

*Credit £0.00.*

'No', she whispers into the night, 'Please work... please...'

Against logic, she presses it again, *Call. No Credit.* Again. *Call. No Credit.*

She drops to her knees, her head falls on her chest, tears well up and she lets out a long sob.

A crunching sound from beyond the open gate. Continuous pressing of gravel stones. Crunch, crunch, crunch. Louder closer.

## *Epithalamium*

Someone coming up the path towards her.

Scarlett looks around in panic. There is a stone bench beside the gate. She dives for it, ducks behind skinning her knees on the rough ground.

A figure appears in the gate, marching in, muttering under his breath. She dare not look, but it sounds like Julian. She hears him walking across the frozen lawn.

'Where is it? Damn it... Damn it! Please, God, this can't be happening... please...'

Scarlett tries to slow her breathing. It sounds so loud to her in the quiet air. Steadily, she peers around the edge of the stone bench.

Julian is pacing up and down the grass, looking down, spinning around frantically. Gun in hand, His breath is fogging the air around him.

*Shit.*

Scarlett looks at the cloud forming around her own lips. It curls around her, rises high over the bench. A beacon of condensing vapour pointing right at her. She takes a deep breath, holds it.

Julian keeps muttering, swearing, pleading to a higher power.

Scarlett's lungs start to burn. She risks a look. He is standing, rubbing his bald head, looking right towards her. She pulls her head back in.

Waits. Lungs crying out for air. She can't breath out. Such a deep exhalation would give away her hiding place immediately. No sound from the lawn. Had he detected her?

Waits. Chest exploding.

A rustle. Scarlett peeks. She sees his back, leaning into the bushes, his hands waving, batting the branches aside, searching for the phone.

Instinct. Or panic. Either way, she is on her feet, diving through the gate, a cloud of breath in her wake.

She doesn't look back as she hurries into the other garden.

Crunch.

She stops as her feet spread the tiny stones noisily apart and immediately leaps onto the grass. She doesn't stop though, keeps running. There is a light at the end of the garden. A car park. A barrier. A road. Keeps running.

\*

The clouds were beginning to thicken. Above her, Scarlett can make out the undulating shapes in the sky above her. Varying grades of grey and blue, tinged with orange from the street-lamps. Flakes are beginning to fall again. Tiny white parachutes, mere millimetres long, were appearing around her. So small that they don't appear to be falling, just floating, drifting ahead of her, swirling as she moves through them.

The paving stones are starting to change colour, from dark grey to lighter shades as fine snow begins to settle like someone has been along with icing sugar and a sieve.

Her arms and legs, exposed to the cold air are beginning to become numb. She can no longer feel her hand on the skin of her upper arms. She might as well have been touching the fabric of her top.

Scarlett looks around to get her bearings. She'd headed

*Epithalamium*

immediately away from the church after hopping over the barrier, skirted a little island of grass and trees, moving up the hill. She'd wanted to get as far away from the man as quickly as possible, deeper into the city, to find people.

What did he want with her? She'd kept asking herself that, over and over. She was perfect? Perfect for what?

He'd made every effort not to kill her, to make it clear that he wasn't going to kill her. He wanted her alive? She'd read about modern slavery, about people being kidnapped and either sold to others or kept in lofts or cellars. Made to work. Abused.

*Abused.*

The word chilled her more than the air every could.

He wanted her alive. What was he going to do to her? Abuse her? Rape her? If he wanted to do it just once, surely he would have done it already. In the alley behind her house. In the car. He wanted to keep her.

Scarlett knew that she was surmising, trying to make sense of the chaos of the events of the last few hours without any real facts. Maybe she didn't want to know. Never wanted to know. If she could get home, get to Chris, tell the police so that they track down and arrest this guy. Maybe she'd never have to find out what he had planned for her.

Chris. How on earth was she going to get there? She had a phone, but it had no credit. The must be a payphone somewhere, but she had no money. She had no pockets. Did they still do reverse charge calls? She hadn't even used a phone box for nearly ten years.

Money. She had none. No, that wasn't true. She'd been paid two

*Epithalamium*

days ago. £800 still in her account after her share of the rent had gone out. A lot of use that was now. She couldn't get to it. She didn't have her card.

Scarlett stopped.

She didn't need her card. A serial online shopper, she had used her card to shop on the internet so many times she had her card details memorized.

She looks around quickly to find herself on a corner. A bistro sits beside her, proclaiming BROWNS in a large golden script, balanced on a hedge. To the left, in a gap between buildings was a main road, Maid Marion Way. It's wide and open and the odd car shoots by.

There were people in those cars, but she wouldn't be able to identify the car until it too saw her. Anyone of them might be the Vectra.

No. Not that way.

Turning right instead, she starts up Park Row. There are some white buildings. All the lights are off, but they have deep doorways.

Scarlett ducks inside one, pushing herself as much into the corner as she can. She holds up the phone, lights up the screen and starts to scroll down the minimal Phone Book entries. Presses Top-Up. holds her breath. It rings once, clicks and a pre-recorded voice starts.

*Your credit balance is zero pounds and zero pence. If you would like to top up, press 1. For -*

Scarlett hits 1 quickly, not waiting for further options.

*To pay by credit or debit card press -*

## *Epithalamium*

She hits 1 again as fast as she can.

A hiss from the road. The sound of an engine, getting louder.

Scarlett looks up, ducks her head. A car passes by. It is silver. Not him.

*Please enter the amount you wish to pay.*

She types in £5. The voice then asks her for her long card number, which she taps in without a pause, followed by her expiry date and finally her CVS number. Her thumbs fly across the keypad with a dexterity that would baffle most of the generation ahead of her but be eclipsed that of the one succeeding her.

*Thank you. Please wait while we verify your payment.*

It is then that an eternity of anxiety begins and passes within seconds she is incapable of feeling.

*Your payment has been successful.*

Scarlett cries out in joy and hangs up. In the same movement, she is hammering a succession of keys that result in the exultant chirrup of another phone ringing.

And it rings.

And it rings.

'Hello?'

Chris' voice makes her voice break before she's even managed to speak. Her words come out too quickly, jumbled, half pronounced, 'Chris, it's me. It's Scarlett, oh shit, Chris..'

'Where the fuck are you?' Chris replies the anger in his voice stinging her.

'Chris - '

'Seriously. It's not fucking funny, Scarlett. Are you in the house?

*Epithalamium*

Been ringing your phone and I find it on charge in the fucking bedroom.'

'Chris!', she shouts down the line, her voice booming down the street. She lowers it, 'Chris, someone took me. I was in the kitchen and - '

'What? Someone took you? What are you on about?'

'I'm in town.'

'What? Notts? What the hell are you doing there?'

'I got away - '

'Hang on, you've got to start again, Scarlett. I don't think I'm hearing you right.'

Scarlett brushes her hair away, trying to think. His voice is filled with anger, irritation, it's making her become confused. He starts to repeat back what she has said to him, a mocking scepticism in his tone that hurts her.

'Please, Chris. Just listen to me - '

'And who's phone is this?'

Scarlet sighs, 'It's his. Chris, just shut the fuck up! Please, get in the van and come get me, I'm on Park Row.'

Silence on the line. Heavy breathing. What's he thinking?

A car engine, tyres moving. Scarlett ducks down. A car goes by. She doesn't get a good look. It might have been the dark blue Vectra. Might not.

A thought occurs to her, 'Chris, is anything going on around there?'

'Here? Like what?'

'Anything. Are the neighbours out? In the alley behind our place?'

## *Epithalamium*

A beat.

'No, nothing's going on. Should there be?'

Scarlett thinks. Should she tell him about Paul? What if he's still alive? What if he needs help? Should she call the emergency services? Should Chris? What if he has to stay to wait for police, or paramedics? She needs him here. Now.

'No. Just, come get me', she states.

'Course, I'm leaving right now, babe'. There is the sound of keys jangling, a coat being put on, 'Are you... are you alright?' His tone is softer now, the information is processed somewhat, genuine concern has found its way into his voice.

Scarlett smiles, 'I'm okay. Just come. Okay?'

'Okay. Just stay on the line though, right?'

'I will'.

Scarlett leans back against the door, rests her head against the cold wood and looks up. He's coming.

The snow is falling thicker, the flakes a little larger. Drifting. The sound of an engine idling.

She turns her head sharply. Behind the parked cars beside her doorway hiding place, another car is on the road, stopped.

The driver is looking at her.

*Epithalamium*

## 8

The exhaust is making a strange noise. Probably from when Julian backed the car in the metal bollard in his haste to get out of the cobblestone car park. All the lights on the back left were now annihilated, with a massive channel cut into the bumper that had clearly dislodged enough of the tailpipe to create a rumbling, clanking sound.
That came after he had torn a good stretch of skin from his forearm trying to climb back over the wall. He had landed hard on the Micra, severely denting the already damaged roof. Back in the car he had thrown it into reverse and gunned the engine. The sudden stop jerked him painfully, enraged him, brought back painful memories of the previous sudden stop he had suffered. The blood on his cheek had dried, but the cold air made the whole side of his face throb painfully.
 A second attempt to escape the confines of the churches car park was more successful and he found himself on Derby Road with a decision to make.
 Left or right.
 Up or down.
 Towards the city, or away.
 There was no telling where had gone, what decision she had made in her attempt to escape him. Surely she would seek out people. Help. The police.
 *God no, please not the police.* That was literally the worst thing that she could do. If they got involved it would be the end of everything.

*Epithalamium*

The end of his world
His own personal apocalypse.
And she has his phone.
Julian has to get her back. Has to get her immediately, before she can make this worse.
Left or right. Decide.
He spins the wheel left, head down the hill towards the city centre. Surely she'll head towards people. He'll shoot straight down to Maid Marion Way, head her off as she tries to cross it into the Square.
His tyres spin on the tarmac as it slowly becomes whiter, providing less friction, less certainty.

\*

The window hums as it is lowered. Scarlett holds her breath, ready to run, or scream, or try to talk.
A voice comes from within, 'Are you her?'
It is timid.
Scarlett says nothing. The phone is still in her hand, by her ear. She can hear the vans engine start, revving; Chris is coming.
The cars interior light comes on. The man inside is not her kidnapper. He is slightly younger, has a long youthful face with clear skin, but like Julian, his hair exists only on the circumference of his head. The pitch black colour of it makes the dome-like scalp almost glow under the cars ceiling light.
His eyes are friendly, but his smile nervous.
'Are you her?' He asks again, 'I'm Daniel.'

*Epithalamium*

Scarlett stands, moves her hair from her face to see him more clearly. She looks around. There are no other cars around, only his, a dark green year 2000 model Astra.

He appears unthreatening, but his question is worrying. Would she be more foolish to get into a car with yet another strange man, or to turn down the chance to not only get out of the cold but to get out of sight of Julian, who was likely still searching for her.

She takes the risk to engage him, 'Am I who?'

He visibly gulps, refers to something out of sight, 'Um, are you... Janet?'

Scarlett frowns, shivers. Fuck, she's cold. She takes a step towards the car, She can feel the heat blasting out through the open window.

Daniel looks at her. He tries to look at her face, but his eyes keep wandering to her attire, trying to work something out. Suddenly, he takes something from beside him and points it at her.

Scarlett jumps, taking an involuntary step back, but it is only a phone. The screen is bright.

'From the App', Daniel continues, 'I'm sure this is right. Park Row, 2 am, Janet. I'm Daniel. Um, are you Janet?'

The car is so inviting. The promise of warmth makes her feel the cold all the more.

Shivering uncontrollably, Scarlet nods and points timidly at the other door.

A smile spreads across Daniels eager face, and he leans over to unlock the passenger door. Scarlett lowers the phone to her thigh and moves towards the car, opens the door. Before getting inside,

## *Epithalamium*

she looks around. A car passes way down on the main road, and a person is walking towards them much farther up the street. Tall, but thin. It looks like a woman. Scarlett ducks inside. The car door slams.

Immediately, her fingertips start to sting with the sudden change in temperature. She breathes out, basking in the relief. She glances at the phone; still connected.

Looking over, Daniel is staring at her, not smiling, but eyes wide. His mouth keeps opening, then closing, then opening again.

Scarlet doesn't move, looks away. She's in the car. In the warmth. Out of sight. *But now what?*

Daniel exhales suddenly and leans toward her, mouth open. Scarlet retract violently, pushing herself into the door. Her reaction takes Daniel by surprise and he pulls away quickly, shaking his head, covering his mouth.

'I'm so sorry, I forgot', he mutters rapidly, 'My friend told me no kissing, but I forgot, and you're so pretty. I'm sorry, I don't know who this works.'

*Good god. Oh shit. The app. This is a hookup.*

Scarlett hopes the terror going through her mind doesn't show. How can this have happened, to have run from one rapist to another. Well, what other kind of people would be out at this time? Is this young man really a rapist? No, not a rapist. Just looking for female company. He doesn't like the type. What exactly does the type look like?

She convulses as the cold leaves her. Hasn't spoken in a while. He is looking more nervous than before. Will he kick her out of the car when he realizes she is not this Janet? Maybe he'll take pity on

## *Epithalamium*

her. Do the right thing. At least let her wait until gets here.

No. Stall. Chris is coming. Fifteen minutes or less. Talk. Stay in the warm, stay out of sight. Chris can deal with this pathetic little pervert when he gets here.

Scarlet braces herself and smiles, ' I'm very cold.'

The sound of her voice obviously settles him. He smiles, turns the strength of the heater up a little bit more, 'Better?'

'Thank you.'

Scarlett rubs her hands together. What next?

Daniel speaks, 'I don't know how this works. Do we go somewhere?'

Fuck.

Scarlett smiles, hoping it appears enigmatic, she's simply buying time, 'Of course.'

'Where?'

'Where do you usually go?'

Daniel smile fades, frowns, starting poking at his phone. 'The app says that you would sort that. Your message, I mean, the one you sent me.'

She gives an affirmative yet non-committal smile. Tries to think. Surely she's seen something on prostitution, a documentary or a story on a soap. Dredges the unused depths of her mind, wading through the muck of discarded information.

'Well, first, we need to-', she speaks slowly, like her words are stuck behind a download bar, buffering, ' - negotiate. We need to talk business before we can... get... down to it.'

She sounds ridiculous. Hopes Daniel buys it. He does and nods, 'Yeah, totally. I mean, I expected this. My friend told me.'

## *Epithalamium*

'Great', Scarlett replies and waits. She glances at the clock on the dashboard. 4 minutes gone. She can do this.

Daniel is looking at her expectantly. She closes her eyes, thinks, 'What is it.. that you want to... do?'

In that moment, Daniel looks as if he might throw up, and Scarlett hope that he will change his mind about the whole thing, but then he looks at her, 'I don't know how much things cost.'

*Things. Shit. What fucking things?* She was by no means a prude; she enjoyed sex, with Chris it is genuinely great. Of her three previous sexual partners, he was the best. She and he were the best together, rather. But when compared to how her workmates spoke, especially Chloe as it happened, Scarlett was comparably uneducated. She knew few phrases and even less how they applied physically.

Faking a confident smile, 'You tell me what you want and I'll tell you how much they cost. Okay?'

That look of imminent nausea and panic return to Daniels youthful face, but to Scarlett's dismay, and with a decidedly apologetic tone. he starts to rapidly reel off his list of requests.

Her mind overwhelmed with the names of the items, and where Daniel cannot remember their names, a vivid description instead, Scarlett tries to maintain an appearance of interest.

Keep going. Chris must only be a few minutes away now. Any moment, his wonderful white van will appear. She'll get in, hold him tighter than she ever has before, and then she'll call the police and tell them everything.

A shape appears at the driver's window and Scarlett's hearts leaps into her throat. It is female. It raps on the glass, making Daniel jump.

He stops listing and describing, winds the window down with the handle, 'Yes?'

'You Daniel?', the woman speaks with a rasp, gifted to her by years of excessive smoking and alcohol. Her face is sharp, her eyes over-large and bulge under arches of tattooed eyebrows. Her lips are thin and hide a surprisingly decent row of teeth. She has yellow blond hair, with dark roots spreading from a defined centre parting.

Daniel shrugs and replies, 'Um, yes?'

She nods, from her shoulder rather than her neck, like a bird. Her eyes flick over to Scarlett, 'I'm Janet.'

Scarlett's heart starts to pound in her chest.

Daniel speaks, 'I'm sorry. You're Janet?'

'Yeah, from the App.'

Daniel shakes his head. His expression unimpressed, doubting, disappointed. Like a small child at first given a bag of Fruit Salad chews, to then have them removed and replaced with Black Jacks. Janet – the real Janet – sees this, 'Problem?'

'No, Um, I - I thought - ', he looks nervously over at Scarlett, who is looking at the clock. It's been over 12 minutes since Chris said he was leaving. She looks at the phone in her hand by her knee. Still connected.

Scarlett quickly puts it to her ear, 'Chris, where are you?'

His voice, sweet in her ear, 'Mansfield Road, just coming by the graveyard. I'll be - '

It cuts off. A Screen appears. *Call Ended.*

A second screen. *Credit £0.00.*

*Epithalamium*

'Chris?', she mutters, looking up.

The appearance of the phone has surprised Daniel, and Janet is glaring at her, 'Just who the fuck are you?'

Scarlett grabs the door handle and steps quickly back out into the cold, but already Janet is hurrying around the bonnet to intercept her with frightening speed.

Scarlett hold up her hand, 'I'm sorry, I just need to wait for my boyfriend!'

'You fucking about with my business?', Janet screams at her, 'Are you seriously trying to steal my business out from under me, you fucking mad bitch?'

Scarlet tries to step away, but her Janet moves with such a ferocity that she is upon her before Scarlett can barely react. Fingers tipped with fake nailed wrap around her hair. Scarlett cries out, her own hand flying out, pushing back.

'Don't you fucking touch me, you cunt!' Janet's' words are venom spat at her. Her other hand rises up, balls into a fist and is driven into Scarlett's eye and cheek.

Sparks fly in her mind, shocking her.

'Please!', she cries out, 'I wasn't stealing your... I was just waiting for my - '

Another impact, her mouth this time, her lip splitting.

'Shut your fucking mouth!, Janet spits at her, 'I don't give a shit what your excuses are; you don't fuck about my business, alright? You getting me?'

'Please, I was taken by a man - '

Janet scoff, 'Oh, fuck off. You listen, I see you around again, I'll fucking do you, you get me? I'll actually kill you, love.' Janet leans in, keeping her claws dug into Scarlett head and face, pressing her into the rear passenger window, 'If I don't suck some dicks tonight, my kids don't eat tomorrow.'

She digs her nail in deeper, a thumb tearing a line down Scarlett's cheek, 'Don't get between a parent and their kids, right?'

Scarlett, her face pressed against the glass, can only look inside at Daniel, his wide terrified eyes. He is unable to help. He doesn't have it in him. It doesn't make him bad. It puts the situation beyond his capacity to deal with it.

Janet's grips let up for a second and Scarlett thinks its over, until the grip suddenly returns and Janet smashes her head back into the frame of the door.

Dazed, Scarlett falls to the ground in a heap.

Janet gets into the Astra's passenger seat and can be heard speaking to Daniel, threatening him with the concept of fulfilling their pre-arranged business or facing alternative consequences. He readily agrees and they drive off.

Scarlett's world is now a small bubble of echoing noise. Her head is pounding, hair stinging, her eye socket and forehead throbbing and sore. The snow falls around her, filling up the world with white, erasing the black ground.

Her mind drifts, exhaustion, fear, and mild-concussion all piling on, her body desiring sleep, to protect itself.

*Chris. He's nearly here.*

No, he is here. She can hear his van rumbling up behind her, the door opening and his boots hitting the ground. He cries out, running to her. Then he is scooping her up in his big arms, taking her away.

*Epithalamium*

To safety.
*Home.*

*Epithalamium*

## 9

Julian watches through the beating wipers as the white van pulled away from the side of the road. It slows at the junction and lethargically turns left along Regent Street. Out of sight.

A moment longer he watches as snow flakes try to settle on the windscreen, only to be relentlessly swept away. Looking over at the passenger's seat, Scarlett's head lolls against her chest. Her eyes lids flutter and her lips part, murmuring. Her lip is cut and a bruise is starting to show below her left eye and the middle of her forehead.

Julian listens. He can no longer hear the van. He turns the key and the Vectras' engine fire up. The headlights flicker on. The tyres growl gently against the increasing layer of snow on the road, pulling the car away.

Julian rolls down Park Row to the same junction as the van, but turns right instead, along Cumberland Place, then left onto Mount Street.

He had gotten to Park Row in time to see that tall woman smash Scarlett's face into the door, and watched with disgust as her attacker had gotten into the car and driven off. What violence. How could someone want to do that to someone else?

Once that car was out of sight, he had pulled up quickly and leaped out to pick Scarlett up. He had expected resistance, but she offered none. In fact, she seemed more than willing to be picked up out of the gathering snow and put back his car. Confused but relieved, Julian had just gotten back in himself when a white van appeared in his rearview mirror.

## *Epithalamium*

He'd pulled away gently and driven as normally as he could to the top of the road where he'd turned around, pulled in and turned everything off.

The white van had stopped near where he had picked Scarlett up. A man had gotten out. Although he was far away down the hill, Julian could see that he was tall and broad, with a beard. He looked around for a few moments, shouted something, then gotten back in his van. The van had then driven off.

Now turning onto Maid Marian Way, Julian was trying to work out what that man was doing? He was a quite a generic look fellow, but there was something familiar about him. Still suffering from his head injuries, it hurt his brain to think too hard.

As overjoyed as he was to find Scarlett again, he almost cried out with delight when he saw the mobile phone lying next to her. He could get things back on track. He could make things right.

As he follows the road to a well-lit roundabout and then doubles back finds the list of Missed Calls, desperate to see if he'd missed any.

His heart stops.

There are no missed calls. But there are several Outgoing Calls to a number he does not recognize.

Julian shoots a rueful look over at the girl beside him.

Goddammit, she'd called someone! How? This phone had no credit. It was for taking calls only.

His head starts to spin. He feels dizzy. Sick. His hands start to shake.

He turns the wheel sharply and tucks the car quickly into an open area, a vehicle entrance to the nearby shopping centre.

## *Epithalamium*

Who the hell had she called?

He thinks about the man who had gotten out of the van. The white van. Big. Bearded.

The memory hits him like a brick. It was the man who had stopped for him earlier. It was this girl's boyfriend. That was who she had called.

He begins to shake his head. This was worse than losing the girl. He screams aloud, starts pummelling his head with his fists.

The noise and movement drags Scarlett out of the stupor, murmuring. Julian stops, grimacing, looks at her. Her eyes drift dreamily up to him, smiling warmly.

Then it fades as he makes sense of what she is seeing. She too starts shaking her head, muttering 'No' over and over. Tears flood her eyes. She is crying, sobbing, like a child, repeated no. No.

The crying becomes louder. He hands come up, she starts to shout.

'Stop it', Julian barks at her, but she cannot hear him over the thundering of her own misery, 'Stop it! Stop it! Stop!'

He reaches over, grabs a wrist, but this makes her worse. She begins to struggle, her racking sobs deafening.

Julian fumbles the gun out of his coat, thrusts it into her face, pressing the cold metal into her cheek, 'Stop! Stop now!'

Scarlett stops, gasping for air. Eyes wide. Not scared. Defiant. She catches her breath enough to hiss, 'You're not going to shoot me.'

Julian bites his bottom lip, driving his teeth deep into the soft flesh, something he does when uncontrollably angry. No reply, no threat comes to him. He can only push the gun deeper into her

*Epithalamium*

cheek, then says, 'Who did you call?'

Scarlett says nothing, but her eyes flick away, thinking, remembering.

Julian waves the phone at her, screaming, 'Who did you call?'

'My boyfriend', Scarlett replies at last, defiance still burning, 'He's coming. He's coming to get me. He's going to *kill you*.'

Fear grips Julian. Not of being attacked by this boyfriend. But of the involvement of the authorities. The chances of this guy finding them were slim, but when he failed to, he was bound to call the police.

Julian exhales, sits back from her, keeping the gun pointed. He tries to think.

The instructions were clear. The consequences of deviating from them clearer still.

He closes his eyes.

Think.

\*

Scarlett watches as Julian closes his eyes. The disappointment of seeing him and not Chris was too much to bear. It was an agony the likes of which she had never before felt, and for a moment she had lost completed control of herself.

Now, her mind was starting to clear again. The fog of her anguish was fading. She was able to think properly again, to observe and calculate. She had escaped once. It can be done again.

Scarlett looked around. They were stationary, beside a road that was quiet, but still had the odd car racing up and down. They were opposite the college, near a shopping centre and the bus station. People. She felt beside her, touched the door. It was locked, but surely she could find the catch, undo it and be out before he had open his eyes and realized.

The gun was still trained on her, but this guy had already proven that he was unwilling to use it on her.

She glances at him. Eyes still closed.

*Do it.*

Scarlett's finger run along the top of the door. Nothing there. She finds the handle; there is an additional button, a switch, beside the lever.

*That's it.*

She tenses herself. Prepares both hands, one finger to push the button, to unlock, the other hand to yank open the door. Then she'd run. Run like hell again. This time she would not be caught.

*Go.*

Scarlett presses and pulls in one swift motion and propels herself at the door.

It doesn't move.

She pushes again, with every bit of strength she has.

Julian speaks, his eyes still closed, 'I am not an idiot. I make mistakes, sure, but never the same one twice.'

He opens his eyes and looks at her. There is no pride in them, just reality, 'Child locks.'

He raises the gun a little, and Scarlett settles back into the seat. Julian looks at her.

Escape. It is the only thing on her mind. She has to get out. Her mind wanders back to Daniel, the young man from the car.

## *Epithalamium*

Gulping, she looks at Julian and says, 'I just want to go home.'
No reply. Just a steady gaze. She continues, 'I will do... whatever you want you me to do... for you. I won't fight, I swear.'
Julian begins to laugh, but she keeps going, 'I'll let you do what you want to me, and I won't stop you, just please afterward, just let me go home and I won't say anything...'
'Stop', Julian says, the laugh fading, 'Just stop talking. That's disgusting... you just... you don't know what you're...'
He breathes out, shaking his head condescendingly, studying her face and finally speaks, holding the phone up as he does, 'How did you call out from this? There's no credit on it?'
Scarlett does not reply. He holds the gun closer, rests the muzzle against her thigh. The metal is freezing against her skin. Scarlett had never more than cut herself accidentally. She knew that a gunshot there would probably not kill her, but she imagined that it would hurt like nothing she had known before.
'I put some on.'
'With what?'
'Money.'
'Don't get cute with me!', Julian bellows, ' Money from where?'
Scarlett replies slowly, not wanting to rile him up more, 'From my bank account. I know my details off by heart. That's how I did it. How I paid.'
Julian stares at her, saying nothing, then suddenly tosses the phone at her. She catches it in her lap, confused.
Julian instructs, 'Put some more on. Now! Do it now!'
Jerked into action, Scarlett does so. The same way she did before. A minute later a screen appears; *Credit £5.00.*

*Epithalamium*

'Done?'
She nods. Julian snatches it back.
'Is there much in your bank account?'
'Um..'
'Answer me!'
'Some, um, about £700.'
'Savings?'
'I don't know... about £500, maybe.'
'Does your boyfriend have online access to your bank account?'
Scarlett frowns, 'What..?'
Julian presses the gun into her leg, prompting a swift answer.
'Yes! Yes, he does!'
'Is there much in his? He has a van; is he self-employed?'
Scarlett nods,
'He has a business account? Is there much in there?'
'Yes, I don't know, please...'
Julian looks away, his eyes focused on the mid-ground, thinking deeply. Then he holds up the phone, presses something, then holds it to his ear.
Scarlett can hear it ringing faintly. Julian looks at her, 'What his name?'
What is he doing?
'Chris.'
Julian nods, thinks, then asks, 'What's yours?'
Silence.
Slowly, she responds, 'Scarlett.'
She doesn't understand what happens next. A sound erupts from his mouth, a gurgle, a gasp. Suddenly his eyes are full of tears and

*Epithalamium*

he frantically wipes them. His eyes bulge as he trying to suppress a sob that bursts out of him. He looks pained as he rubs his eyes, trying to clear them, catch his breath, regain control.
A little voice.
'Scarlett? Hello? Scarlett!'
Julian coughs, clears his throat, and puts the phone to his ear, 'Is that Chris?'
Scarlett strains, but cannot clearly make out the other half of the conversation. Chris sounds angry, she can hear that much, maybe even upset. She's never seen him upset. Never seen him cry. Like nothing could make him cry.
Julian interrupts Chris tirade. He has adopted a more confident delivery, like he's selling insurance over the phone, 'I have... your girlfriend... here with me, Chris. She wants to come home. Let's talk money, and see if we can make that happen, shall we?'

*Epithalamium*

## 10

They wait.

The snow is falling heavy now, filling the air. The flake are huge and can be measured in centimetres, not just millimetres. They settle on everything that rests even somewhat parallel with the sky. Roads are disappearing, becoming indistinguishable from the pavement. Pitch roofs turn white. Parked cars are fading away little by little.

Scarlett watches as the window screen of the car becomes periodically opaque. They are cleared by the wipers, activated manually at random by Julian, as and when he feels that his field of vision is too restricted.

The engine is off, but the key is turned until the electrics alone are on. It allows control of the wipers, but the heaters are not blowing, and the headlights are off.

Julian keeps looking in the rearview mirror, as randomly as he uses the wipers, or even checks the phone for calls.

They are parked at the side of Cliff Road, wedged between what was 2 cars, but are now becoming unidentifiable mounds of snow. Facing away from the back of the Broadmarsh shopping center, open, undeveloped land on the right, and the titular cliff on the left towering several stories over them.

Hot breath curls from Scarlett's mouth and she shivers. Her mind takes her to back to Chloe smoking her cigarette in front of the Golf Club, much to the envy of Scarlett. Christ, that seemed so long ago. She glanced at the clock on the dashboard.

03.16 am.

## *Epithalamium*

It was only about 3 hours ago.

Where would Chloe be now? Asleep, no doubt. Warm in her bed. At home. Safe.

She too will be soon, when Chris arrives with whatever sum of money he and Julian had discussed. She hated that this disgusting man had managed to extort money out of Chris. Not just Chris, his business. The company he had built from nothing, which although kept them afloat, had never truly broken even.

Scarlett wonders how much. Julian had not said.

'He's here', Julian spoke, his voice high. The confidence from the phone conversation had ebbed away, 'When I open your door, get out slowly and don't move. Alright?'

Scarlett nods, 'And you'll let me go?'

Julian removes the keys from the ignition. He opens the door, steps a foot out into the snow and looks back at her, 'I said slowly, Really slowly.' then he gets out fully, slams the door.

Scarlett watches him walk around the bonnet, his eyes fixed on her, the gun in his hand. When he gets to her door, he reaches out and opens it quickly, the gun pointed at her.

She gets out slowly. Still shoeless, the snow crunches underfoot and the cold stings her feet. She moves away from the door, allowing Julian to close the door.

Scarlett looks down the road, a thin meadow of white with spikes of darkness thrusting skyward, orange flares burning at their peaks.

There is no one there.

Where is he?

Julian uses the gun to motion from behind her. She turns. A

*Epithalamium*

hundred yards away, where the dark rock of the cliff meets the sheer windowless brick sides of the shopping centre, under the tram bridge that spans the wide gap, stands a lone figure.

She smiles, even when she feels the cold metal prodding her shoulder, forcing her to walk.

The hundred yards between them seems like a hundred miles. Every step makes her bare feet cry out in pain, and she feels herself starting to limp as the pain increases.

Closer, she can start to make out his features. His broad shoulders, his long legs. His scruffy hair and beard. It's definitely him.

But there is no grin. That boyish, mischievous grin is nowhere to be seen. A grimace takes its place. Joy, fury, and fear are etched on Chris' face as he watched Scarlett approach. Small and barely dressed, shivering, limping; her face bruised and bleeding, drained of colour, tired.

She knows she must look a mess. She knows Chris' almost obsessive compulsion to protect her, even from trivial rivalries at work. This would be killing him. Unable to act. Powerless. Impotent. Emasculated.

Julian must see his face, because he suddenly grabs Scarlett, snakes his arm around her neck, pulls her back to him.

Chris reacts, stepping forward from under the bridge into the snowfall, stops quickly when Julian waves the gun and shouts, 'I have this, Chris.'

Chris exhales, long and slow, his fists clenched. He calls out.
'Babe, are you hurt?'
She smiles, happy to see him, to hear him. Nods. 'I'm okay.'

*Epithalamium*

Chris frowns, points at his face, meaning hers; her bruises. She shakes her head, 'This wasn't him. It was - '

'Enough', Julian interrupts, 'She's not hurt. I haven't hurt her, at least not half as much as she's caused me injury, as you can see.' Julian angles his battered cheek for effect.

Chris holds his hand apart, 'Okay whatever, mate. I just want my girlfriend back. Please. Here - ' He reaches inside his jacket, and Julian cannot help but turn the gun on him. Chris slows, takes a plastic carrier bag out of his inside pocket, holding it up.

Scarlett watches as he unfolds the rustling bag, exposing its contents. Piles of notes, loose, they look like twenties, dozens and dozens of them. How much would that be?

'That's as much as I could withdraw, but like I said, I can transfer the rest to you', Chris explains carefully, but his usually solid voice is shaking, 'I can do it right now. Please, let me do it and let me take Scarlett home.'

Julian closes his eyes suddenly, emotion making him tremble. A sharp intake of breath from him, 'Did you call the police?'

Chris shakes his head firmly, 'No. Definitely not.'

'*Did* you call the police?', Julian asks again, shouting this time.

'No! I wouldn't call them, mate. I wouldn't trust the fuckers. Not with her life'.'

Scarlett knows he means it. She means everything to him. She can feel it. Barely 5 yards separates them, and yet she had never felt closer to him than in that moment.

5 yards. Nearly home.

Julian speaks again, 'Do you promise? No police?'

Chris lowers his voice, slows it, 'I swear to you.'

*Epithalamium*

Julian nods. He seems to believe him.

Chris holds out the carrier bag with one hand, holds another out to Scarlett.

'Please.'

Julian is now shaking a lot. The gun drops a little. His arm around Scarlett's neck loosens.

The air is still. Snow swirls. Time doesn't move.

The gunshot is the same as it was with Paul, but the shock of it means that Scarlett cannot take it in like she did with her unloved neighbour.

She feels like the bullet has hit *her* in the chest, ripping her heart into shreds. Tears fill her eyes so that she cannot see as Chris falls backward into the deepening snow. The carrier bag full of money

And she is being pulled away. She struggles with everything she has left. Her top rips a little, freeing her. She tumbles forward, towards Chris's prone form. Throws herself at him reaches out but she is stopped.

Hands yanks her away before her own can make contact with the man who loves her. Her head jerks forwards under the impact of a fist, dazing her, but still, she fights. Her heels drag painfully across the ground.

Chris gets smaller and smaller until he is nothing but a dark smudge on an untouched canvas.

\*

Scarlett is screaming when Julian tries to force her inside the car's passenger door. As she kicks out at the door frame, he presses his

## *Epithalamium*

hand over her mouth. She bites him. He lets go. She screams again, her shrill cry echoing off the side of the cliff, projecting across the open ground.

Panic grips him, give him strength. He yanks her away from the car, swings her around and throws her down against the wheel, into the snow.

He drops on her, pinning her with his weight. She struggle, pushes the door shut, in so doing, revealing the tiny form of Chris lying under the tram bridge. She cries through gritted teeth as she stares.

Julian pushes the gun into her cheek. She looks up at him, locks eyes and pushes her face back at him. Daring him to pull the trigger. To do what he has so far refused to. Wanting him to. Begging him too.

He can't think of anything to say to her. Threats seem empty, lies would not be believed now. He feels as impotent now as he did at the beginning of this hellish night.

All he can do is hold her still as she bucks under him, staring at him with eyes filled with fury.

He looks back at the body in the snow, but it is not alone now. Another figure is there, walking tentatively out across the gap between the steps that lead up to the Lace Market and the centre's entrance. It looks around, making sure it is safe before it goes to Chris.

Scarlett is watching too. It calms her.

Julian seizes the chance, pulls Scarlett up to her feet. He opens the door and she allows herself to be put in the seat. Door closes.

He dashes around and once inside starts the engine and pulls

## *Epithalamium*

away.

Although he keeps the gun pointed at her as he drives. Scarlett does nothing expect stares silently into the side view mirror. Even when the car rounds the corner and joins the main road, she neither talks nor moves.

In silence, Julian takes the car out onto Canal Street to the roundabout and turns right along London Road, before making a left onto Cattle Market Road. It is very quiet around here, and he takes another left, into the Cattle Market itself. A labyrinth of cobblestone streets and ageing low-slung warehouses.

He stops the car and takes some deep breaths.

All he can do now is wait.

He has done all he can.

Still, Scarlett says nothing. He doesn't trust it. As diminutive and pathetic as she looks, she has proven to be far more trouble than he'd ever thought she could be. Her drive to survive this was astonishing. More than his own? What was he doing? What he had done... was going to do?

Julian ceased that train of thought. It could lead nowhere good.

Please, god... let this be over.

As if intervened by divinity, the mobile phone rings. It chirrups loudly in the small, silent space. Only now does Scarlett look over.

Julian stares at the flashing screen, seemingly unable to takes this final, irreversible step. His thumb manages to find the button. The ringing stops. He puts it to his ear. His own voice is small, 'Hello?'

'Where have you been?'

## *Epithalamium*

'I had... I'm sorry. I'm so sorry.'
'Shut up. Do you have it?'
Julian looks over at Scarlett, 'I have it.'
'Is it a good one?'
Julian closes his eyes, swallows hard, 'Yes.'
'Did it give you any trouble?'
'It was... okay. Please, tell me where.'
Silence. Julian waits at first, but the silence is torturous, 'Hello? Hello!'
'Do not shout at me.'
'I'm sorry, please, I'm sorry. Just... please, I'm begging you... please, let me finish this. I'll meet you anywhere.'
'Yes, you will. But first, answer me honestly, Julian. Did you leave any breadcrumbs?'
Julian voices trembles, 'No.'
'Don't lie to me.'
'Nothing. I... I cleared everything up. There are no... breadcrumbs. I swear to you.'
There is a long inhalation. Musing. Debating. Julian heart beats in his chest with painful ferocity.
'A60 south. Between Bradmore and Bunny, there is a right turn. Take it. Follow it for 1 mile. There's a red gate and a field. 1 hour.'
A bleep as the caller cut the connection.
Julian looks at the phone in his lap as the light fades and shuts off, going into standby. For a beautiful second, he forgets about Scarlett beside him, until she speaks.
'Who was that?'

*Epithalamium*

## 11

Scarlett felt a momentary conflict as she watched the exchange on the phone. She could only hear one side of the conversation, but it had given her an insight into what this nightmare might really be about.

When Chris had fallen away from her, and the white around him had begun to turn crimson, she felt the whole essence of what she thought life was drop out from beneath her. She had tumbled into a void she didn't even know existed. An existence with meaning. No way forward, no way backward. An infinite present, stretching out before her. A black, putrid landscape without a horizon.

And she had fought, but not for survival. Not anymore. She wanted to follow him, to make this foul man lose his temper and kill her too. But he hadn't. He had resisted. Her life was more important to him than she realized, but she no longer cared why. Make him take it. That would be her revenge against him.

But then the door had swung shut, revealing her man. Alone in the cold snow. And an angel standing over him.

A splinter of hope penetrated her heart.

She had let Julian incarcerate her in the car once more and watched in the mirror as the person knelt down and touched Chris. She saw that person put what appeared to be a phone to her ear. Maybe just the police, but perhaps an ambulance.

Then, just before the car turned and she lost sight, the person had begun to presses rhythmically on Chris' chest.

She had felt her heart burst, and the desire to live that she had

## *Epithalamium*

lost, had returned tenfold.

Julian had been looking at the road. He had not noticed. He was sure Chris was dead, but Scarlett knew that there was at least a chance that he was not.

She had resolved that she would do anything to get home.

*Anything.*

She sat in the car now, in the dead silence of the Cattle Market, after hearing that phone call. This man was scared, terrified of something. He was not in control.

She asks again, 'Who was that?'

Julian says nothing. He moves the gun in his hands, staring at it. Scarlett licks her lips, chooses her words, 'Do you know what you've done? Who you killed?'

No reply.

'He was my whole life. He was my future. He was my family.'

Julian scoffs loudly, spits his reply, 'Family! He wasn't your family. He was just a – he wasn't family. You don't know what family is, you stupid girl. That's not family... it's not...'

He was shaking his head vigorously, 'You do anything for family. You die for them.'

A beat.

Scarlett says, 'Chris died for me.'

Julian looks over at her. His eyes search hers.

She continues, 'Chris came for me. To take me home. Back to our life together. And you killed him. You killed my family. You're scum.'

'No!', Julian screams, thrusting the gun at her, 'No! I'm not! I'm not like that! I'm nobody! I don't do this!'

## *Epithalamium*

'You've killed 2 people!'
'I had to!'
'Why?'
'To keep them safe!'
'Who?'

Julian backs away a little, looking away, the gun not moving. Scarlett leans forward, towards Julian, towards the gun, 'Who was on the phone?'

Julian's face goes red. His eyes bulge. His teeth clench as he tries to hold back the flood of emotion that bubbles barely below the surface. Finally, he lets out a long rattling exhalation, followed by a tumble of words, 'The man with the clown mask.'

Scarlett frowns. She didn't expect answer like that.

Julian gaze fades. He is no longer in the present. He's in another place, another time. He continues slowly, 'He took them after we visited Lisa's mother. We were driving down from Rufford, on one the long roads that cuts through the woods and he comes racing up after us in a BMW. I just thought he was going to overtake, but he came up alongside us and started to push us towards the side of the road. We were doing about fifty. I had no choice, I had to slow. He nosed in front of us, making up stop. Then he was out, with a gun shouting... he had this mask on. A grinning clown, oh God. They were screaming, Lisa and... my daughter... they were so scared. I was terrified. He hit me and dragged them out. He threw a bag at me, told me if I called the police that he'd break their legs and arms and leave them in the woods.'

Julian stops for breath. His hands are shaking violently, tears

*Epithalamium*

pouring from his eyes, 'She's so small. She's 6, but she's the shortest in her class. And so innocent. She has a unicorn. A little plastic thing; cheap rubbish, from a claw game we played on in Yarmouth... she talks to it. Jesus Christ, she's so delicate.'

He twists the gun, wrings it, and Scarlett's heart starts to thud, fearing he could let it off without realizing.

'I sat there for I don't know how long', Julian says, 'I didn't know what to do. Call the police, don't call them. Wait here, go somewhere. I vomited. I remember that. But he called. There was the phone in the bag he threw at me, and this gun too.

'He said that he wanted a girl... a young woman. He wanted me to get her and bring her to him. If I refused he would kill my family. If I contacted the police or alerted them in any way he would kill them. But he... he said more than kill... he said he'd... he said he rape my wife and he'd...'

He stops, buries his face in his hands, shaking his head as if trying to dislodge those thoughts, send them falling away into obscurity, 'I asked what girl. He said any. I said I needed to know. He said a nice one. I'd know when I saw her. I had no idea. I assumed he just attractive, but not just pretty... nice too. You looked nice.'

Julian looks up at her, 'I don't want to do this. Not to anybody. I have no choice. I have to get my family back. I don't know what he's done to them, been doing to them... I have to get them back. I have to get them home. And I'm sorry, I need you to do that.'

Scarlett says nothing. She has no reason to believe any of this. It's far more likely to be a lie. A new way to placate her, to subdue her. To make her feel sympathy for his plight; it's not his fault, he's being forced into it. She asks, 'What does he want to do with me?'

Julian looks at her sadly, 'I don't know. I really don't.'

Scarlett inhales, closes her eyes.

Home.

*Chris.*

She forces these things to the front of her mind before she speaks again, 'Does it have to be me?'

Julian frowns, 'What?'

'He asked for a girl. Any girl. A nice one. A pretty one. It doesn't have to be me, does it?'

'I tried for hours. You were the only one that was right, that I could get.'

'But it doesn't have to be me.'

'It is you. I'm sorry.'

Scarlett reaches out suddenly, put her hand on his hand, squeezes it. She braces her self, swallows nausea at having to touch this man, 'What if I could get you another girl?'

Julian shakes his head, 'I've had the call. We have to go.'

'Please, I have a life. I'm a good person. I've done nothing wrong. I don't deserve this!'

Julian pulls his hand away, 'I don't deserve this either! My wife doesn't deserve this and my daughter certainly doesn't... but it's happened and they are far more important to me than you are!'

Scarlett grabs at his arm, 'But please, if you don't care about me, then it doesn't have to be me! It can be someone else! Please, I can help you get another one. Someone else. Someone who doesn't matter. Take her, please... then let me go home.'

*Epithalamium*

Julian shakes his head, 'There's not enough time.'

'Please. Please. There is. I know someone. I can get her. I can get her to come to us, and you can take her and I can go home. She won't be missed. I promise you.'

A pause, perhaps a consideration of the awful pitch.

'Why this girl? Is she pretty?', Julian asks.

'Yes, Blonde, slim. But she's a bitch. If anyone deserves this, it's her. It's not me. Please?'

Julian looks at her, at her hands clutching at his arm, at her tearful, pleading eyes.

'Please.'

*Epithalamium*

## 12

The sky is heavy with snow, and the ground is thick with it. The sodium orange light from the street-lamps bounce off the white ground and back at the sky, and the other way around. It is eerily bright, no shadows. Just lightness everywhere. Night has gone, but it is not day either. An in-between. A strange nothingness.

Scarlett can see her trudging through the snow towards them. Head down, bowed against the squall blowing about her. Flakes scatter ahead of her, her blonde hair swirling with them. Dancing. Leading her on. Lining her path.

She sits in the back of the car, behind the passenger seat, as low as she can, peaking out between the gaps in the headrest. The girl advances alone. Snow covers North Sherwood Street. The only indication of where the road ends the pavement begins is the cars that line the curb, them self barely anything more than mounds.

Julian breaths heavily but slowly in the driver seat. The gun is held low, out of sight. He watches her, seemingly more nervous than her.

It had taken Scarlett several more tries to convince him to do this. Finally, it seemed, her desperation had beaten him. He had accepted the idea, and in so doing had convinced her that he was not the disgusting, vile man that she had come to believe that he was. Julian was simply as desperate as she was. As willing to do anything to see his family safe again as she was to get out of this and to see if Chris truly was still alive.

Could she really do this? To substitute herself for some other person. To send another girl to whatever horrible fate had awaited

## Epithalamium

her?

*Yes. She could.*

Scarlett did not deserve this. This person did.

Janet crosses the road to them, struggling in the snow and uneven surface in her tall heels. She had changed her clothes since attacking Scarlett and driving off, leaving her to the mercy of Julian. The very sight of her made Scarlett blood boil. How could Janet had been so evil to her, when all she needed was help? If she had just helped her, Scarlett would not have to be doing this now.

Scarlett repeats this to herself, over and over.

The phone lay under the handbrake. It usefulness now expired.

Julian, after initially agreeing to the substitution, had almost changed his mind when Scarlett told him how she was going to get the girl to meet them. He felt it was complicated, with too many variables, but he had eventually let her use the phone.

She had downloaded the same App that the young pervert Daniel had been using and spent a few minutes tracking Janet's profile down, before sending her a message that she hoped would attract her. It was simplistic but crude, and the offer of good money was laid out.

5 minutes had passed, with Julian becoming increasingly agitated, but finally, Janet had replied with a time and a location. Clearly, she had finished with Daniel.

Scarlett tenses herself. She couldn't bring herself to fully believe what she was doing. This wasn't her. She had never done, or even dreamt of doing, anything resembling this. It was horrific. Immoral.

No. Think of Chris. Thinking of finding him at the hospital.

## *Epithalamium*

Sitting by him until he wakes up. Think of his face when he sees her.

Janet is almost upon them. Scarlett slips lower, staying out of sight.

There is a tap on the window, and Julian lowers it.

'You Gary?' the voice drifts inside. Julian had not wanted to use his real, name, with Scarlett then realized she did not know or care to know.

Julian nods, 'Yeah. Are you Janet?'

The girl laughs, 'No, sorry, I'm Fiona.'

Scarlett frowns. Fiona? Had she changed her name?

Easing herself up, she peers through the gap at the girl leaning in through the passenger window. Slim, a round face, silver-blond hair, small chin and brown, almost piggishly small eyes.

'Janet couldn't make it', the girl, Fiona, continued, her voice high, sing-song, 'She asked me to come see you instead. Will I do ?'

She leans away from the window, hanging on, showing off her wares in a saggy low-cut top. Her smile is warm, but there is a sadness behind it. Her eyes are genuine, a kindness there. She is young. Naive. Scarlett stares at her,

It's not Janet. It's some other girl. A young girl. Janet was pushing her mid-thirties, this girl was not even twenty,

Julian nods, gulps nervously, 'Yeah, you'll do fine. Thank you. Please, get in out of the cold.'

Fiona smiles, opens the door, 'Thanks. My nipple are like - '

She stops. She is looking directly at Scarlett.

There are no shadows. There is light everywhere.

## *Epithalamium*

'What the fucks this?', Fiona demands, 'I was told just you. What you playing at? I don't do girls.'

Julian holds out his hand, 'Please, just wait.'

'No, I'm out.'

Fiona moves to push the door shut, but Scarlett has already moved, so abruptly it surprises herself. She springs from the back seat, twisting herself between the seat and grabbing at Fiona.

Surprised, the young girl cries out. Scarlett finger wrap around her thin jacket. Fiona pulls away, but she only serves to pull Scarlett out of the door.

Scarlett crashes painfully into the snow and the hard ground below. Fiona screams, kicks out, struggling away. Scarlett grabs again, finding anything, pulling at her jacket, her top. They thrash in the drift, Fiona heaving herself away, Scarlett clawing at her.

*Where is Julian? Why isn't he helping?*

Fiona continues to scream. The whole street is filled with her shrieks.

Scarlett finally manages to find grip under her bare feet, lunges forward, grabs onto Fiona's hair, but the girl has found her own friction. Twisting her body, she launches a fist at Scarlett's face. It crashes into her nose. Blood gushes. Blinded, Scarlett lets go.

Only now is she aware of Julian, standing over her, pointing the gun.

Her vision swimming, Scarlett can only see Fiona's feet disappear over a small wall and her vanishes down a narrow alleyway between two terraced houses. Julian follows, steps into the alleyway and is gone.

## *Epithalamium*

Their footsteps echo, fading away into silence.
Nothing then.
Scarlett, her face on fire, forces herself to stand.
She is alone on the street.
*Alone.*
Quickly, she starts to move, dragging her feet painful through the snow, clutching her face. Blood pours between her fingers, leaving a stark trail behind her.

Poor girl. She doesn't deserve this. It should have been Janet.

The thought is in her mind suddenly. She banishes it. The girl is gone, Julian is gone. The deal is done. She is free.

It should have been Janet. *If I don't suck some dicks tonight, my kids don't eat tomorrow.* The words of the violent prostitute come to her suddenly. Janet would have been missed. Her kids would have been waiting for her. What would have happened to them without their mother coming back? No, she was bad for them. They'd have been better off without her.

Her own mother came to mind. She was a bitter, self-centred woman at times, but she couldn't imagine how she'd feel if her mother had been taken away like that.

Better this way. Better Janet didn't come.

Maybe Fiona wasn't as young and innocent as she looked.

Maybe -

'Stop!' Julian's voice thundered over to her.

Scarlett didn't stop but did turn to look, to see Julian, with Fiona cowed at his feet.

But Julian was alone.

'I said stop!'

## *Epithalamium*

Scarlett shook her head, kept going. Limping on. *Home.*

Footsteps behind her. She keeps going. She won't stop. She would die before she let herself be put back in that car.

Her hair is pulled, but she pulls back. A male cry of anger and frustration and suddenly Scarlett was flying forwards instead. She falls into the snow and suddenly Julian is standing over her, gun and all.

She screams at him, 'Where is she? We agreed! Her, not me!'

Julian replies, 'I couldn't catch her. I'm sorry.'

Scarlett can't believe what she is hearing. Not after everything. She cries back at him, 'We'll get another! We have time!'

'No, there's no more time. We have to go.'

He reaches down to her, but she fights him off, 'Please! Let's call the police now then! They can help! They will! You can't do this.'

Julian shrugs. He looks calm now, resigned, beaten, 'I can. Because I have no choice. I am sorry, I wanted it to be her, not you. You're right; you don't deserve this. But when does anyone deserve anything bad that happens to them? I was a good man. A charted surveyor of all mediocre things. I work in an office. But there's no happy ending for me after this, and I'm okay with that, so long as my family is alive. I've given up on fairness. All I have left is hope.'

Scarlett shakes her head furiously, 'No. I'm not going. I'm not going to let you.'

Julian raises the gun, but she bats it away. She can see herself in the hospital, with Chris. She can see her hot shower. Her clean, warm clothes. Days, maybe weeks, waiting for Chris to come home. But he does. And they drink wine, have sex and lie in bed

*Epithalamium*

and watch crap on Netflix.

'You need me alive. I'm going home because you're not going to shoot me.'

But he does.

Julian aims the gun at her thigh and pulls the trigger.

*Epithalamium*

## 13

It has stopped snowing and the temperature is climbing rapidly. It's turning the delicate blanket of untouched whiteness to a grey slush that bunches up at the sides of roads that are now rivers of viscous water.

Julian drives as quickly as he dares along the long winding stretch of the A60 that twists away to the south, past endless pale fields and spurs of dark farmhouses. He passes the odd car, but not many, and he pays them at little mind as they pay him.

The sky is less dark now. The clouds still hang heavy, but a long fracture has broken in them in to. A Jagged line, like someone has been scratching at the walls of night with torn fingernails until, finally, a pallid light can cautiously enter.

A bend and a few houses rise up around him, flying past as he exceeds the 30mph limit by 15. Thick, watery ice splashes up around like a wake, and in only a few seconds he has cleared the village of Bradmore.

Julian looks over at the passenger seat, at Scarlett who heads knocks against the window as his tyres rattle over the badly kept rural road surface. Her eyes are closed, her lips slightly open as she breathes softly. She looks peacefully asleep, instead passed out through exhaustion and blood loss. Her thigh is a mess of it, both dried and fresh. A tourniquet made of a blanket Julian had on the back seat wrapped around it.

She looks pale and fragile. Her shocking red hair, once neat and brushed straight is now a twisted, knotted mass, framing a discolored eye and a nose that sports a cut on the bridge and thin trail of red beneath it.

*Nearly there. Nearly done.*

Julian slows the car, looking for the turn. He can see rooftops in the ahead distance and begins to panic, fearing he's somehow missed it, but it comes up. A pair of willow trees guards the entrance to a dirt track that leads away from the main road, out across the fields.

The sudden bump as he moves from even tarmac to undulant frozen soil jolts Scarlett awake. He glances over, sees her blank look. Watches with a weight in his chest as the awareness seeps into her. The disappointment, the sadness, the defeat.

The car judders along painfully, rocking the suspension in a manner that this model is not used to, on and on, deeper into the white nothingness that spreads out on either side.

The red gate is stark against the snow caped trees and the ground. Julian slows and pulls in, winds through a copse of trees.

He slams on the breaks.

The light in the sky is still pathetic, the fields and the trees are clinging to their shadows. The strongest source of illumination is that projected from Julian's car and the vehicle before them.

Julian lets his breath out slowly, squinting against the glaring yellow headlights, before releasing the clutch and easing his Vectra forwards until he is about 10 yards from the other.

Changing the angle, Julian can now see the other vehicle clearly. It is an old Mercedes van, dirty yellow with a 2-door cab and an open flatbed with lows sides. There is a blue tarpaulin across the top, sides down with hooked bungee cords.

'Please don't do this', Scarlett whispers, but there is no power in

## *Epithalamium*

her voice anymore. Just a repeated line, a phrase that has lost all meaning.

Julian makes himself ignore her and waits. He dares not move in case getting out is the wrong thing to do, and simultaneously panics in case it isn't.

The driver's doors of the van open and someone steps out into the deep, unblemished snow. He is tall, with broad shoulders and narrow waist. He wears blue stonewashed jeans and a thick green Parka, open to reveal a bare chest beneath. His face is covered with a rubber mask.

A clown grins back at Julian, a slash of a mouth that stretches from ear to ear in a grotesquely drastic curve. In contrast to the manic smile, a single tear falls from eyes that are angled down to the centre, surprised eyebrows arching above them. A visage of happiness, fear, sadness, and anger are all expressed at once.

The man in the clown mask stands silently for a second, then reaches back inside, takes something out and cradles it in arms. Long, thin, tapered. A hunting rifle. He takes a few steps forward, raises the rifle, projecting it from his hip, waves the end.

'Get out.'

Julian takes a massive inwards breath and gets out, the gun in one hand, dragging the keys out of the ignition with the other.

'Hold the gun by the handle.' The man in the clown mask's voice booms across the open expanse.

Slowly, Julian manoeuvrers the pistol so that he is holding the grip it by his fingers, praying that this is what he meant.

'Come here.'

Julian's heart is pounding. His legs feel weak. He genuinely feels

*Epithalamium*

that he might fall, but knows he can't. Somehow he has to see this through. As he walks closer, he looks at the van. Where are they? Oh, god... please let the man in the clown mask be true to his word. He's no reason to trust him but has no choice except to.

The man in the clown mask says nothing until Julian is a few feet away, then speaks. His voice is deep, gruff and his accent broad, southern, London perhaps. 'Give me the gun. You don't need it anymore.'

Julian holds it up. It is taken. He is now unarmed yet doesn't feel more defenseless than before.

Silence. The clown mask. The hunting rifle. The rustle of trees in the breeze. The pounding of his heart. Daybreak.

'Any loose ends?'

Julian shakes his head vigorously.

'Did you have to use this?' He raises the pistol at Julian, finger on the trigger.

Julian gulps, nods.

'Did you enjoy it?'

Julian closes his eyes, squeezing out tears. He has forced himself not to think of the people he has had to shoot tonight, afraid that if seeing them as people would break his resolve. And he needed every ounce of courage he could muster. He had very little to begin with. Now, with those words *did you enjoy it*, the weight of his actions crept into his mind.

The man in the clown mask jerks his head towards the Vectra, 'Let's see it then. What did you bring me?'

Julian frown, mouth open. This is it. Oh Jesus, forgive me, this is it. He cannot move. His legs are frozen, his mind locked.

## *Epithalamium*

He can't do it.
He has to.
*He must.*

He must give this innocent young woman whom he doesn't know to this man in exchange for his family whom he loves with all his heart.

There is no choice. Why won't his legs work? He's come this far, why can't he finish it?

The man in the clown mask cocks his head, then screams, his low voice suddenly high, 'Show it to me!'

Jolted into action, reminded, he supposes of what is at stake Julian scuttles away to the passenger side of the car. He pulls at the handle, the door opens a little, then slams shut.

Scarlett is pulling at it from the far side, shaking her head.

'Please!' It is Julian shouting at her, pulling at the door vigorously, 'Please!'

Finally, the door flies open and Scarlett dives away, but Julian grabs her feet, yanking her out. Once outside, her wounds prohibit her from fighting, and Julian drags her along by her arms, towards the man in the clown mask.

Scarlett is dropped by his feet and Julian immediately steps back, like a cat presenting as owner with a half dead bird.

Julian feels sick. As if he might vomit at any second. His chest is throbbing, his stomach a knot. He watches as the man in the clown mask looks down at the barely dressed girl, running his hidden eyes over her, cocking his head, muttering to himself.

Suddenly, the man in the clown mask drops to his knee, reaches out. Terrified, Scarlett flinches as the big hand touches her face,

*Epithalamium*

runs a finger along her cheek.

'You must be freezing', the clown mask says, 'Have this.'

The man in the clown mask pulls the big Parka of his shoulder, exposing his naked torso. He is muscular and lean, his arms and chest are awash with scars of various kinds. Some are long and deep badly healed, other are mere circles, barely there anymore. There is a long line across his throat, reddish but long healed.

He drapes the coat around her shoulders. She is clearly out of her mind with terror, but is too weak to say or do anything now, and lets it happen.

Julian watches as the man in the clown mask nods and he hopes it is with approval. The man then leans close to Scarlett's and whispers something.

The silent monologue is long and Scarlett nods several times during it, cries too, tears running down her face until finally, the man in the clown mask stands, pulling Scarlett up with him.

Together, they turn and walk towards the yellow van. Julian watches nervously as the man in the clown mask opens the door for Scarlett, and helps her climb inside. Once settled in the seat, she bows her head and looks into her lap. The man says something to her, she nods and he closes the door.

He then walks around to the driver's door.

Julian heart leaps, he steps forward, 'Wait! Wait! My family! You said you'd give them back to me! You promised!'

The man in the clown mask ignore him, opens the driver's door. Julian is now screaming, pleading, his eyes wide with fear,' Where are they!? Where is my family!' Give them back to me!' He drops to his knees in the snow, his head pressed together in his lap.

*Epithalamium*

The man in the clown mask reaches into the cab, to the steering wheel. A rattle and the van's engine comes on. A loud humming. The heaters.

The man in the clown mask steps back. He closes the door and stares at Julian for a moment, then walks to the back of the van, to the flatbed.

Struggling to catch his breath, Julian stares as, one by one, the man in the clown mask unhooks the bungee cords until the rearmost panel is free. He then pulls the locks and the panel flops down.

Julian cannot see what is happening at the rear. He cannot move from his knees, frozen by fear what was about to be revealed to him.

The man in the clown mask pulls two things from the flatbed, from under the blue tarpaulin. They crash into the snow.

One is large, one is small.

*Epithalamium*

## 14

Julian can barely see through his tears as the man in the clown mask drags the two inert figures towards him. They are tied, hands and feet bound, mouths gagged. Their clothes have been changed. The attire is unfamiliar, and at first, he can't make sense of it, but as they are dragged closer, he can see they are dresses. Lilac, with flowing pleated skirts and straps with white flowers sewn on. In their hands are bouquets of flowers, stuck to them with black tape.

He can't breathe. His lungs are closing up. He is shaking so hard he can feel brain rattling in his skull.

The man in the clown mask stops when he stood over Julian, and drops the ropes, letting the two sag to the ground. After a moment, he steps away, walks back to the van.

Julian's gaze drops to the forms.

Two pairs of wide eyes stare back at him.

Julian heart breaks. He lets out a wail of agony.

Two pairs of eyes blink.

He freezes. Did he imagine that? He leans in, their beautiful eyes track him and he lets out a cry of relief.

Julian touches them both, as they look up at him, tears in both their eyes. Such is his shock and joy that he doesn't know what to do for a second.

Untie them. Take out their gags. Who first? Oh, god…

Julian fumbles between them, before taking out his wife's first. She gaps for air, and immediately says, 'Untie her first, Julian!'

Julian pulls out his daughter's gag, then his fingers tear away the

## *Epithalamium*

bizarre bouquet, tug desperately at the knots at her hands. As soon as they are free, she throws her little arms around his neck, squeezing him. He hugs her back, tighter than he thinks he had ever done before. He unties her feet, then, with his daughter still attached, starts on his wife's hands.

Once they are free, Karen grabs at Julian, pulls him close, then starts on her own feet.

Julian lost in the joy of being reunited with this family, has forgotten about the van. It is still there, the engine still running. The man in the clown mask is now sat in the driver's seat, door closed, staring down at them. Scarlett is beside him. Her head is down, but her eyes look up from beneath the Parka hood, at Julian.

'Come on', Karen says, pulling at Julian, 'Come on!'

It is her who pulls Julian up. Exhaustion has overcome him. It is Karen who yanks at him, telling him to pick their little girl up.

Together they tumble through the snow, back to the car. Julian opens the car door, bundles his daughter inside the back. Karen gets in after her, puts her arms around her.

Julian, his head spinning, gets in, starts the engine. He looks at Karen, 'Are you okay? Are you hurt?'

Karen, her voice trembling, perhaps with relief, rather than fear, doesn't answer, 'Who is that girl?'

The question takes him off guard. Follows her gaze to the young woman, sitting motionlessly, head bowed, in the van. He cannot answer her. Cannot find the words.

'Is that what he wanted? In return for us?' Karen persists.

Julian gulps, looks at his daughter, who looks back at him with

*Epithalamium*

wide, tear-streaked eyes.

'Julian! Who is that?'

'I don't know, Karen. I don't know!'

Karen looks out at the van. It hasn't moved yet. It is waiting for them to go first.

Julian starts the engine, 'We have to go.'

The car starts to reverse. Karen, holding her daughter tight, keep looking back at the van. 'What did you do, Julian? Who the fuck is that?'

Julian shakes his head, 'I don't know. He told me to get someone, I got someone and he gave me you back. I had to do it. I had to get you back. I had to save you.'

'What is he going to do to her?'

'I don't know, dammit!' Julian shouts, 'I don't know. I don't want to know!'

He keeps reversing, the engine whining, the tyres squelching in the melting snow. 'Did he hurt you? Did he hurt Scarlett?'

Julian looks at his daughter, his own Scarlett, so small and fragile in her mother's arms. When he looks at her, he is convinced he's done the right thing. Karen has not answered.

'Karen? Did he hurt her?'

After a moment, Karen replies, 'He didn't touch Scarlett.'

'But, those clothes? Did he? What are they?'

'Bridesmaid dresses. He made us change... I don't know why.'

'Did he..?'

'No. I changed Scarlett. He didn't touch her. I swear Now, Julian, where the fuck did you get that girl?'

Julian brings the car to stop, turns in around and starts to drive

## *Epithalamium*

back along the dirt track, towards the main road. The sky is brightening, the heavy clouds drifting away. Diffuse red light is gradually filling the sky.

'Karen, please. I did what I had to do. She's no one, Karen. No one. She has to be no one otherwise I'll lose my mind, do you understand?'

He looks into her eyes, pleading with her. She is frowning, torn. She holds Scarlett closer. Julian looks at Karen, 'Did he... did he hurt you?'

Karen looks him in the eyes, recalling painful memories, but says firmly, 'We'll talk at home, Julian, please. I'll tell you everything, but first, we need to get Scarlett home.'

Julian closes his eyes briefly, clenches his teeth, then nods slowly.

He felt dizzy.

Everything he has done that night.

Everything he heinous act had carried out.

Every living person he had, in his mind, reduced to a comfortable facelessness.

The screams of his wife and daughter as they were taken, were now replaced with those of the strangers he had sacrificed in place of those he loved.

They would never leave him. They would echo in his mind endlessly.

Karen speaks again. Her tone is soft, soothing. It is the voice he once fell in love with, that is supposed to love him, but there is an implication of words, for now, left unsaid.

'Take us home.'

*Epithalamium*

# epithalamium
/ˌɛpɪθəˈleɪmiəm/
*noun*

(/ˌɛpɪθəˈleɪmiəm/; Latin form of Greek ἐπιθαλάμιον *epithalamion* from ἐπί *epi* "upon," and θάλαμος *thalamos* nuptial chamber) is a poem written specifically for the bride on the way to her marital chamber

Printed in Great Britain
by Amazon